Street Siren

Tom Batt

CHAPTER 1

The city was silent. Lights twinkled in the dark like the stars in the night sky. The hard windowsill wasn't exactly comfortable, but it allowed Devlin to relax as she admired the view. She drew on a cigarette, blowing the billowing smoke out the open window, the soft wind taking it away. As she pulled the burning stub from her full lips, her blood-stained hand was shaking, a charm bracelet slipping down her arm.

Although she was skinny and wore nothing more than lingerie, she was immune to the cold. Her mind was on other things. Her eyes were glazed over, blood dripping from her face. She flicked the cigarette butt out of the window and slipped off the sill with ease. As she made her way across the studio apartment, she glanced over at the carnage she was responsible for only a few moments ago. His head was almost gone, and what remained was unidentifiable. His naked body was drenched in blood, soaking the silk bed sheets beneath. There was a spray of red up the headboard and wall. Devlin entered the bathroom, flicking on the bright light. She twisted on the tap, and the water splashed down heavy, ricocheting off the bowl.

The blood washed from her hands as she scrubbed them furiously to remove every last trace. She splashed some of the water over her face to remove the red staining clinging to her skin. Each drop was a reminder of what she had done, cast aside as if to erase the crime.

As she stared into the mirror, her dark eyes reflected back at her upon the face of a demon she no longer recognised. She reached up and pulled a blonde wig from her head to reveal brunette hair with pink streaks through it on one side. There was the girl she knew. Her tired appearance betrayed her young age of only twenty-two.

Suddenly, nausea overcame her, and she turned to the nearby toilet. The vomit burned her throat. She had not eaten in a while, so it was mostly bile laced with red wine.

She picked up a crumpled cocktail dress from the floor and slipped it over her hips, zipping it up tight. She then threw on a leather jacket and collected her handbag before stepping out to view the bloodbath again. Devlin couldn't help but stare at the hideous sight once more. A sense of relief washed over her. She picked up the stained hammer from the blood-soaked carpet and wiped it down with the bedsheet. She placed it back inside her handbag and slung the strap over her shoulder. Her eye was drawn to a brown leather wallet sitting on the bedside table next to a mirror with lines of cocaine on its surface. As it flipped open, a large wad of notes wedged inside revealed itself. She plucked them out and shoved them into her pocket, tossing the wallet back onto the table. She then headed for the front door and quietly pulled it open, taking one last look back at the scene before ducking out into the darkness.

CHAPTER 2

Several weeks earlier, Devlin could never have predicted the killer she would become. She opened her eyes wide and looked around the expensive hotel room. She was lying in a large bed, silk sheets draped over her slender naked body. The sound of snoring startled her, causing her focus to shift to her side, where a large hairy man lay asleep next to her. She pulled a face of disgust before pulling back the covers and slipping carefully off the bed so as not to wake him.

She hastily got dressed and pulled on a pair of black ankle boots, still admiring the room. She still hadn't gotten used to the level of luxury her clients bathed her in. The night before, she didn't have a chance to appreciate it, but now in the broad light of day, she soaked it all in. She wondered how much the room must have cost for the night. She charged a lot for her services, so she was curious as to how much these men were spending in total. *I guess to some men, money is no object*, she thought.

Out of the corner of her eye, she glimpsed a bulging envelope standing proudly against the gold-leafed bedside table lamp. She collected it and stuffed it into her small handbag, the paper making a rustling sound as it crumpled. The sleeping giant stirred, and she froze. She was reluctant to wake the beast lest he requested more services from her. For most clients, she would take a deep breath and oblige without too much discomfort, but to sleep with this particular man took a different kind of courage. As far as she was concerned, last night was enough. The snoring continued allowing her to relax again.

4

Devlin slipped on her leather jacket and crept through the room, her boots silent on the soft shag carpeting. She slipped out the door pulling it quietly behind her.

#

Her journey home on the tube was an uneventful one. Usually, she would have to deal with the many commuters staring at her, questioning her profession or the yuppies leering, but today was Saturday, and she could avoid that awkwardness. She was still feeling a little groggy and hungover, so she spread out on the seats and took a little power nap. The gentle swaying of the carriage helped lull her to sleep.

Devlin arrived back at her modest studio apartment in Camden and kicked off her boots. It was a tidy abode well-decorated with modern art prints on the walls by Patrick Nagel and David Hockney. A large bookshelf on one side of the wall contained the many classics of the 19th and 20th centuries, all tatty and worn from multiple readings. The furniture seemed second-hand, as if bought from car-boot sales or found on the street, but together they gave a certain charm to the place.

Devlin made her way over to a small scratched and dented dining table where a young woman sat hunched, scribbling on a sketch pad. Roxy was only twenty-five, but she had the face of someone who had seen it all. Her hair was tied back in a ponytail, and she wore jogging bottoms and a T-shirt, a comfort she appreciated when not working.

It didn't matter they'd been living together for two years; Devlin still enjoyed coming home and finding her waiting. It felt good to know she would always be there for her.

Roxy glanced up from her doodling and smiled briefly.

'Hey, how was your night?' she asked, returning her focus to the pad.

'It was fine,' Devlin replied, plucking the envelope of cash from her handbag and placing it in front of Roxy.

Roxy put down the pencil and snatched up the envelope. Flicking through the notes, she seemed impressed by the amount.

Devlin had already moved over to the sink in a small kitchenette and filled a glass with water. She gulped it down with relish. She was parched. She hadn't drunk since the night before, and that was two vodka cokes and a glass of wine. The cool refreshing liquid slid down her throat, and she let out a gasp of relief.

Devlin watched as Roxy took the envelope over to an unmade double bed. She reached under and pulled out an old metal cigar tin. As she flipped open the lid, a bunch of notes sprung up, almost spilling out. She squashed them back down, placing the new load on top. Devlin couldn't help but smirk as Roxy had trouble closing the lid again. Eventually, she managed to seal the tin and slid it back under the bed.

'We're going to need a bigger tin,' Devlin said, still sipping at the water.

'If you keep earning like you do, we will,' Roxy replied, returning to the table.

For a moment, Devlin was going to raise the issue of opening a bank account again but knew it would fall on deaf ears. Roxy didn't trust banks and was insistent the money would not leave the apartment unless it was to be spent.

'How was your night, anyway?' Devlin asked.

'Another weirdo with a foot fetish,' Roxy replied, exasperated as she sat back down.

Devlin scrunched up her face before finishing up the last of the water in the glass. The clients with fetishes were always the worst. The more bizarre they got, the harder it was to say yes, but they were the ones always willing to pay whatever it took, so it was just as hard to say no.

Roxy laughed at Devlin's face of disgust. 'Yep, my thoughts exactly. Still, he paid good money. Plus, I have lovely feet, so it's not that big of a deal.'

Devlin grinned. Roxy always knew how to slip a compliment to herself into a conversation. It was one of her personality traits that Devlin loved. No matter what they were talking about, Roxy would always get it in somehow, and it made Devlin laugh when she did. The stranger the conversation, the harder she laughed.

'I'm going to take a shower,' Devlin said, placing the glass in the sink. She headed over to a bathroom door tucked toward the back of the apartment. Roxy picked up the pencil and continued to draw.

#

When Devlin had finished in the shower, she came bursting out of the room and almost made Roxy jump out of her skin. She thought something terrible had happened, but her fears were proven to be wrong when Devlin danced around the room wearing only a towel, singing along to Kim Wilde's *You Keep Me Hangin' On* using a hairbrush as a microphone. The music was emanating loudly from the bathroom, filling the rest of the flat alongside a plume of steam.

At first, Roxy didn't know how to react, but when Devlin approached her and leaned in close, shutting her eyes and singing passionately, Roxy couldn't help but burst out laughing in amusement.

Devlin ignored the laughter and doubled down, stepping onto the bed and turning it into a stage.

Roxy was now on her feet, clapping along with cheers and whistles. Devlin bounced on the bed so hard there was a risk the slats would break and she and the mattress would sink through.

When the song ended, Devlin finished with a pose. Legs apart, one hand on her hip, the other extended into the air, still clutching the hairbrush. Roxy clapped and whooped as Devlin bowed. She jumped off the bed, giggling, and hugged Roxy.

'You've got an amazing voice. You should consider singing professionally,' Roxy said.

'Don't be silly,' Devlin replied, raising an eyebrow, though deep inside, she was buzzing from the compliment.

'Who knows, if you're successful enough, you could one day be living the dream.'

'You're the only dream I need.'

Devlin kissed Roxy softly on her lips, tasting her cherry lip gloss.

'Aww, aren't you sweet? I think I might throw up,' Roxy said with a smirk.

Devlin laughed, punching Roxy playfully on the arm.

'So, what do you think?' Roxy asked, gesturing toward the sketch pad on the dining table.

Devlin raised her eyebrows at the stylised image of a rose. She reached out and picked up the pad for a closer inspection.

'Never mind me singing professionally. You should be an artist.'

'You like it?' Roxy asked, slightly unsure if Devlin was mocking her.

'I think it's beautiful. You're really going to do it then?'

'Of course I am. But I'm going to need you by my side holding my hand, so hurry up and get dressed.'

Roxy slapped Devlin on the bottom.

'All right, I'm moving,' Devlin said, giggling as she returned to the bathroom.

CHAPTER 3

It was a busy night at their favourite local bar in Camden Town. The weekend had arrived, and everyone was out looking for a good time. Devlin and Roxy sat by the window, each with a glass of rosé.

'Let me see it again,' Devlin asked.

Roxy leant to one side, pulling down her skirt slightly to expose the medical dressing on her hip. She peeled back the gauze pad to reveal a tattoo of the rose she drew. Devlin cocked her head to get a better view.

'It looks so good,' Devlin said.

'Why don't you get one?' Roxy asked, replacing the dressing.

'I don't think I could handle the pain.'

'It didn't hurt that much.'

'Your face said otherwise.'

Roxy laughed. 'Was it that obvious?' She took a sip of her wine. 'I think it would be sexy on you. You have this innocent girl look, but when guys see the tattoo, they'll think you have a dark side.'

'I'll think about it,' Devlin said, hoping Roxy wouldn't bring it up again. As much as she liked the look of a tattoo, the pain was something she could never handle, no matter how minor, and Roxy's took at least an hour.

A car horn from outside caught their attention. Roxy glanced over at the black '87 BMW 7 series parked at the side of the road.

'I guess that's my new trick,' she said, collecting her handbag.

'Why doesn't he come in?'

'Apparently, he's too shy to meet in public.'

'Aww, that's sweet.'

'I don't think his wife would think that,' Roxy smirked, sliding off her stool.

'How do you know he's married?'

'Think about it. Why else wouldn't he want to meet in public? He doesn't want to get caught.'

Devlin collected her handbag and followed Roxy out of the bar pulling on her jacket.

Devlin glanced over at the driver as they stepped outside, but his face was shrouded in shadow. She was about to step closer for a clearer look, but Roxy's voice interrupted her.

'I'll see you tomorrow,' Roxy said, planting a kiss on Devlin's cheek. 'Love you.'

'Love you too. Have a good night.'

'I always do,' Roxy grinned as she backed up toward the car. As she neared the passenger side, she spun around and leant in through the open window. Devlin watched as a few words were exchanged before Roxy climbed in. She gave a brief wave to Devlin, and then the car drove off. Devlin waved back half-heartedly.

#

Devlin tossed and turned in bed, eventually waking. It had been a bad night's sleep. It always was when she knew Roxy was somewhere else, with someone else. She looked at the digital alarm clock. It was 11:30 a.m. She rolled over to the other side, expecting to find Roxy lying next to her, but she wasn't. Devlin reached out and ran her hand along the undisturbed bedsheet, a look of confusion on her face.

She sat up, assuming Roxy was already awake, but the apartment was empty of another soul. Devlin pulled back the duvet and slipped off the bed. Her bare feet tiptoed across the cold hardwood flooring toward an answering machine hooked up to a phone. Perhaps Roxy had left a message to say she would be late home, but there was no display of new messages. This wasn't like Roxy. She always got home before 10 am and if she was held up, she would let Devlin know. A horrible twisting pain came from within her gut.

The police station was unusually quiet. Devlin entered nervously, looking around, unsure where to go. She approached the front desk but found no uniformed officer there to greet her. Instead, there was a tall thin man in a grey suit with his back toward her rummaging through filing cabinets.

'Excuse me,' she whispered.

Detective Sergeant Lewis Weyland turned around to reveal his kind face sporting a well-groomed moustache. He was one of a handful of detective sergeants in his late twenties, having excelled at the academy and quickly risen through the ranks of the Metropolitan Police Service. He glanced around, expecting there to be someone to help this girl, but when it became clear there wasn't anyone, he approached the desk.

'Uh, can I help?' he asked with a stutter.

'I'd like to report my friend missing. She didn't come home, and I haven't heard from her,' Devlin struggled to say.

'Um, okay. When did you last see her?'

'Last night.'

'Okay, and you expected her to be home by now?'

Devlin simply nodded.

'Well, we don't normally file a missing persons report until it's been twenty-four hours. Chances are, she's lost track of time. Nine times out of ten, that's usually the case. If I were you, I'd go home and wait for her. I'm sure she'll show up,' Lewis said with a comforting smile.

'Okay,' Devlin replied, letting her head drop. She turned around and headed for the exit. Lewis watched her with sorrowful eyes and realised he hadn't given this girl what she wanted. She was scared for her friend's safety, and his words hadn't helped subside that.

'Wait,' he called out.

Devlin stopped and turned to him, her eyes hopeful again.

'What's your name?'

'Devlin. Devlin Hunter.'

'Well, Miss Hunter, why don't you give me her description? I'll let units in the area know and get back to you if I hear anything,' Lewis said, collecting a pen from a pot and finding a scrap piece of paper.

Devlin forced a smile and returned to the desk, leaning upon it.

'She's about my height, twenty-five years old, with dark hair and brown eyes.'

Lewis scribbled down the information, but at the same time, he was mesmerised by this girl. Her big beautiful blue eyes, rosy red cheeks and full lips hypnotised him as she spoke. He always considered himself a knight in shining armour and couldn't resist a damsel in distress. He just hoped he could help her.

CHAPTER 4

The old man was in his sixties, and rheumatoid arthritis was making it difficult to walk these days, but he would suffer the pain for his much-loved canine companion, Lacey. Their walks in the quiet open grasslands of Hampstead heath were the highlight of his day. Watching her bound about chasing squirrels allowed him to live vicariously through her.

He sat down on a bench and took a much-needed rest, sipping at the bottle of water he had brought with him. It was a short-lived rest, however, as Lacey began barking. She very rarely barked unless in distress, and this concerned him. He pulled himself to his feet and approached her as quickly as his legs could.

'What is it, girl?' he called.

He found Lacey nestled in amongst some long grass, and as he neared her, he caught a glimpse of what had disturbed the dog. He stepped closer for a better look and felt his jaw drop in horror.

'Jesus,' he whispered.

Protruding from the ground was a pale, blood-stained hand.

#

The police had the area cordoned off with tape as forensic officers collected evidence and took photos. A couple of officers were struggling to keep back morbid onlookers keen to get a glimmer of the corpse.

A rundown 1982 Ford Cortina pulled up not far from the crime scene. Lewis climbed out of the passenger side and looked over at the commotion building. Detective Chief Inspector Mitchell Grantham appeared from the driver's side. A short dumpy man a year from retirement, he scratched his full grey beard before running a hand across his balding head. He frowned at the crowd gathering by the tape, causing problems for the officers. He never understood the fascination people had with dead bodies.

'Get those bloody people away from the crime scene. If they don't comply, arrest them!' he shouted with frustration. The last thing he wanted was any potential evidence contaminated by gawkers.

Lewis followed Grantham toward the crime scene and ducked under the police tape. Lewis turned away in disgust at the mutilated body that lay before them, exhumed from a shallow grave. There were broken bones, bruising and gashes across her skin, and the clinging dirt giving it a rough texture. Her glassy white eyes were wide open, staring up at them, peaking through straggling hair across her face.

'Are you all right?' Grantham asked, slightly amused.

'Yeah, just a shock,' Lewis replied, trying to collect himself.

'They certainly made a bloody mess of her,' Grantham said, crouching down for a closer look. He was aware of a uniformed officer standing by him with a notepad and pen in his hands. 'ID?' he asked without taking his eyes off the body.

'No, sir,' the uniformed officer replied. 'We believe that's her handbag down there.'

Grantham looked over to where the officer was pointing to find a small handbag located by the corpse. It had been buried with her, dirt staining the white material.

Grantham pulled a latex glove from his pocket and stretched it over his thick fingers. He slid the handbag closer and rummaged through the contents.

'She's a prostitute,' he surmised with confidence.

'What makes you say that?' Lewis asked.

Grantham glanced up at him. 'How many women do you know who carry ten condoms in their handbag?'

Lewis was impressed by the quick deduction, although it did feel too presumptuous. He wanted to question the theory and put forth possible alternatives, but experience taught him never to undermine his superior. He returned his focus to Grantham's search of the handbag. His partner plucked out a small photograph of Devlin and Roxy smiling in a warm embrace.

'Well, at least that's someone who'll know who she is,' Grantham said, passing the photograph up to Lewis.

'I know this girl,' Lewis said, looking at Devlin in the photo. 'She came into the station this morning. Reported her friend missing.'

Grantham stands, snapping off the latex glove.

'Congratulations. You just found her.'

Grantham patted Lewis on the shoulder and headed over to a forensic officer. Lewis continued to stare at the photo. He thought Devlin had such a nice smile, and yet he wondered if she would ever smile again after hearing of her friend's death.

Looking past the photo, something on the ground caught his eye. A charm bracelet weaving amongst the grass by the body. Lewis removed a pen from his pocket and used it to pick up the gold jewellery. He studied it with interest. *I guess these charms ran out of luck*, he thought.

CHAPTER 5

Devlin hadn't been able to do much since reporting Roxy missing. She didn't feel like eating, and she couldn't sleep. She paced around the room, biting her nails, praying that any moment her friend would come through the door and she could finally calm down.

When a knock came, Devlin's heart began pounding as she rushed over to answer the door.

'Roxy?' she said as she whipped open the door.

Unfortunately, it was not Roxy. Lewis stood before her, looking forlorn. He was awkwardly tugging at the sleeve of his coat. Devlin stared at him, confused, and he suspected she didn't remember his face.

'Hi, I'm D.S. Weyland,' he said, hastily taking out his ID and showing her. 'You came into the station this morning to report your friend missing.'

'Have you found her?'

'I'm sorry to say we've found a body. We believe it may be your friend, but to confirm, we'll need you to identify her,' Lewis said, trying to maintain a sensitive manner. He was well aware of how people could react in these situations, and he wanted to ensure he approached this correctly.

Devlin shook her head. She was speechless. This is what she dreaded, and now it was all coming true.

#

The coroner's room was cold, sterile and uninviting. Only the dead could feel comfortable. Devlin and Lewis were stood by a window, the view blocked by a curtain. Devlin hugged herself as she waited impatiently. Suddenly, the curtain parted, revealing a body on the other side of the table covered in a white sheet.

The coroner approached the body and pulled back the sheet from the head to expose the battered and bruised face. Devlin threw up a hand to her face in shock at the horrendous sight before her. She couldn't believe that was a person lying before her, or at least used to be.

'Is it her?' Lewis asked.

Devlin shook her head. 'I don't know. I can't tell.'

'Does she have any distinguishing marks? Tattoos? Birthmarks?' he said, keen to get this over with as quickly as possible.

'She has a tattoo of a rose on her right hip,' Devlin stammered to say. A part of her didn't want to say so they could never fully prove it was Roxy, and she could believe she was still alive.

Lewis knocked on the glass, and the sharp sound made Devlin jump.

'Can you show us the right hip?' Lewis shouted so the sound could reverberate through.

The coroner nodded and pulled back the sheet from the hip to reveal a rose tattoo, the very same as Roxy's.

Devlin couldn't contain herself any longer. That was it. There was no doubt Roxy was dead. Her legs buckled beneath her, and she almost hit the floor, but Lewis was quick to react, catching her fall. He held her close as she screamed out in tears.

#

Devlin stared at the white wall opposite her in the waiting room. She was perched on an uncomfortable plastic chair, her eyes red and raw, tears still running down her face. Her mind was trying to wrap itself around all this. How could Roxy be dead? Why would someone kill her? She hoped this was all a nightmare and she would wake up soon.

Lewis sidled up beside her with a plastic cup of water. He handed it to her and sat down. Devlin took a sip of the water, but it tasted bitter to her. Everything did now.

'I'd like to ask you a few questions if that's okay?' Lewis said quietly.

Devlin took a deep breath and nodded.

Lewis reached into his coat pocket and took out a small notepad and pen.

'You said the last time you saw her was last night. What time?'

'About nine.'

Lewis made a note on his pad.

'We have reason to believe she was a prostitute. Is that correct?'

'Call girl,' Devlin snapped back.

'Excuse me?' Lewis asked, his brow furrowed.

Devlin looked up at him with a slight scowl.

'*We* are call girls, not prostitutes.' Devlin turned away, realising her words. 'Roxy *was* a call girl.'

'I didn't realise there was a difference.'

'We don't stand around on street corners. So yeah, there's a difference.'

'I'm sorry, I didn't mean to offend.'

The last thing Lewis wanted to do was upset this girl even more. He needed her to cooperate, and he was very close to blowing it.

'She was picked up by a trick in his car the last time I saw her,' Devlin said.

Lewis was relieved to know he hadn't ruined his chance.

'A trick? You mean a customer?' he asked. He was never good with street slang.

Devlin nodded.

'Someone she's been with before?' he continued.

'No, she said he was new.'

'Did you see his face?' Lewis said, ready to continue writing.

Devlin shook her head. 'It was too dark.'

Lewis was disappointed. He hoped Devlin would have information that could solve this case quickly, but it wasn't going to be that easy.

'Do you remember what type of car it was?'

Devlin closed her eyes, trying to picture it in her head, but it wouldn't come to her. 'No, I'm sorry.'

Devlin felt the tears burgeoning, and Lewis knew he had pushed her too far too soon. She needed time to grieve and process everything.

'I think that's enough for now,' he said, pocketing the notepad.

Lewis reached into another pocket and took out a small evidence bag containing the charm bracelet he found. He removed it from the plastic and admired the many charms. Devlin caught sight of it from the corner of her eye.

'We've already checked this for prints. I thought maybe you'd want it,' he said, holding it out to her.

Devlin took the bracelet and studied it. The last time she saw it, it was dangling from Roxy's wrist. She slid it over her own.

'Thank you,' she said, taking another deep breath to hold back the tears.

'If you ever need to talk,' he said.

'I know.'

'Are you going to be okay tonight?'

'I'll be fine.'

'We'll find who did this, Devlin. I promise.'

Devlin looked up at him and forced a smile. She then turned her focus back to the bracelet, hoping he wouldn't break that promise.

CHAPTER 6

Reese loved his job; he couldn't think of anything better. He spent most of the day burning through the many films the rental store had to offer via a TV tucked under the checkout desk. He was halfway through the explosions and carnage of *Lethal Weapon* when he was interrupted by Devlin entering the store.

Surprised to see her, he slid his feet off the desk, snatched up the remote and pressed pause.

'Devlin Hunter, as I live and breathe. I haven't seen you in a while,' he said with a wide grin beneath his wispy bum-fluff moustache.

'Are you still selling?' she asked.

'Am I still selling? Is Brooke Shields the sexiest girl on the planet?'

Devlin stared at him, unamused by his comedic attitude. Reese could see she was in no mood for games and dropped the act. He ran his fingers through his bleach blonde mullet.

'Yeah, I'm still selling. What do you need?'

'The usual.'

'Coming up,' he said with a sly wink. He was about to head into a backroom when he paused and turned. 'Do you need any utensils?' he added.

Devlin replied with a nod.

He disappeared into the back room, and the sound of rustling could be heard. Devlin waited impatiently, scanning the VHS tapes stacked on the shelves. The sound of the fluorescent lights buzzing above her reminded her of those at the coroner's. Reese returned with a brown paper bag. He placed it on the counter.

'Same price as before.'

Devlin took a wad of notes from her jacket pocket and counted through them. Reese was stunned by the amount of cash she had and questioned in his head how she must have earned it. She passed a few notes over to him, and he counted to check it was correct.

'It's always nice to have a customer return. Enjoy,' he said with a smile.

Devlin snatched the brown paper bag off the desk and shoved it in her handbag. She rushed out of the store, allowing Reese to return to his film.

#

The orange flame of the lighter burned the underside of the old spoon, leaving a scorched mark beneath. The liquid nestled in the concave cradle bubbled as the heat passed through. The thin point of a needle dipped into the liquid and vacuumed up every last drop containing it inside a narrow chamber, ready to be discharged. Devlin tightened a belt around her upper arm, then tapped at a vein to make it rise. She took up the syringe and pressed it deep into the bulbous channel, squeezing the plunger to pump the poisonous contents into her bloodstream. After withdrawing the needle, she loosened the belt, allowing the drug to make its way around her body. She fell back onto the bed and relaxed, the syringe slipping from her fingers. A faint smile appeared on her face as she closed her eyes. She fiddled with the bracelet around her wrist, lost in memories of Roxy.

#

Devlin couldn't remember how long she'd been living on the streets since running away from home not long after turning sixteen. Growing up with an abusive mother was no picnic, and so as soon as she felt confident enough, she packed a rucksack and set off into the world alone.

Months went by of finding shop doorways to sleep in and bins to scavenge leftover food from. It wasn't exactly the life improvement she imagined, but at least she was free of that witch.

She met another homeless teen runaway called Snorky. He'd been surviving on his wits for several years and became a wealth of tips and advice for her. He soon invited her to join him and his friends at an old house they were squatting in. The place was decrepit and stunk, but it was warm and dry, and that's all that mattered to Devlin. They had developed a small community amongst themselves, helping each other and contributing what skills they had to better their communal life. They also shared a penchant for narcotics.

Snorky introduced Devlin to heroin, and it gave her the relief she was longing for all her life. It took away the pain and suffering and lifted her. Her addiction grew quickly, and she became a slave to its pleasure.

Then one day, the police raided the house, and she was one of only a few who managed to escape arrest. She found herself back to square one, walking the streets and looking for a place to sleep. On top of that, she now had an urge that needed satisfying, and she had no way of pleasing it.

Devlin was sat on a bench in the park, scratching her arm, wondering how she was going to get her next fix. It was so cold her denim jacket could hardly keep her warm enough. She thought it was only a matter of time before she died on the streets. She even considered going back home. And then Roxy approached from out of nowhere. She didn't know what to think at first. Why was this girl coming up to her and saying hello? She'd lost so much faith in people that she was sure Roxy was going to hurt her. She asked Devlin her name, and she reluctantly told her.

'Interesting name,' she said. 'You look like you could do with a warm place to stay, Devlin. I've got more than enough room.'

Roxy held out a friendly hand and smiled softly, but Devlin still wasn't sure what to do or think. A cold wind blew right through her, and she decided *what the hell? Nothing could be worse than suffering out here.* Devlin took her hand and walked with her. Roxy threw a comforting arm around her, and that was it. *She saved my life that night, that much I do know,* Devlin thought. And now she was gone.

CHAPTER 7

The large basement walls were lined with shelves containing thousands of VHS tapes stacked neatly, each one labelled and in order. Derek Whitbread, a suave gentleman in his fifties, sat with legs crossed on a leather sofa in the centre of the room with a glass of whiskey in his fat hand. He wore a branded polo shirt and beige chinos, an outfit he considered comfortable home wear.

A projector displayed a film on a clear white wall in front of him. The glow of the screen lit up his entertained face. He took a sip of his whiskey and believed at this moment he was truly happy.

The sound of the front doorbell interrupted his peace, and he felt irritated. Just when he was perfectly relaxed, someone had to disturb him. He placed the whiskey glass down on the coffee table in front of him and paused the projector before heading upstairs.

He hobbled through the large hallways of the manor house using a wooden cane to support his weight. There was a slight limp in his left leg, the result of an unfortunate polo accident in his youth. He passed a collection of antiques and ancient treasures, filling the corridors like a museum. They were the spoils of his father's adventures throughout the world at many others' expense. And the apple didn't fall far from the tree.

Before he could answer the door, there was a loud knock, and a voice came through from the other side.

'Mr Whitbread, it's the police. Open the door.'

Derek stopped in his tracks and panicked. His heart began pounding in his chest. This was it. The day he had always dreaded. They discovered his secret. He backed away from the door as the knocking increased, then turned and bolted into the study.

Derek took a key from his trouser pocket and unlocked the top drawer of his desk, yanking it open. He pulled a handgun out just as the sound of the front door being broken open made him jump. Police officers led by two plain-clothes detectives rushed into the house. The two detectives stepped into the study to find Derek with the gun pointing at them. They froze, raising their hands in defence.

'Put the gun down, Mr Whitbread,' one of the detectives said calmly.

Derek shook his head. He put the barrel of the gun to his temple and pulled the trigger. The gunshot echoed around the room, and bits of brain and blood splattered onto a hung painting by J. M. W. Turner, another treasure obtained by his father using underhanded means. The detectives watched on in horror as Derek's body collapsed to the ground, a pool of blood forming around him.

'Someone call an ambulance!' shouted a detective. 'The rest of you search the house.'

Even after Derek's body had been taken away, officers were still searching the house several hours later. They had finally made their way down into the basement and were scanning the many VHS tapes on display. One of the officers nudged the projector, and it continued playing on the screen. The officer turned to view the film and was horrified by the images blown up on the screen.

'Jesus Christ,' he said, attracting the attention of the other men in the room. 'Is that real?' he asked, hoping to God someone would tell him it wasn't.

Another officer pressed stop on the connected VHS player and ejected the tape. A red "X" was marked on the label.

CHAPTER 8

Lewis could feel the headache coming on. He had spent the last hour staring down at his desk at a collection of documents trying to find the smallest speck of a clue to give them a lead. He rubbed his temples in an attempt to massage his brain into action. The clutter around the office wasn't helping. He didn't like mess; it made it difficult for him to think. Unfortunately, he shared a room with Grantham, a notoriously untidy man.

A VHS tape in a plastic evidence bag dropped down in front of his eye-line. He looked up to find Grantham standing before him, clutching a polystyrene cup of tea in his hand. Lewis picked up the tape and studied the red 'X' on the label.

'What's this?' he asked.

Grantham pulled up a chair and sat down opposite Lewis, gently placing his cup on the desk.

'The home of a suspected paedophile was raided last night. Shot himself. Most likely from guilt or shame, whatever the fuck you want to call it. Coward's way out if you ask me.' Grantham paused to take a sip of his tea. Lewis waited impatiently. 'Anyway, that tape was found in his possession.'

'So? Why are you telling me this?'

'You might want to take a look at what's on it,' Grantham said.

#

Devlin lay in bed, the covers pulled tight over her. The curtains were closed, but the bright sunlight forced its way through the thin material. Devlin's face was suffering the combined effects of crying and drugs. What little make-up she still had on from days prior was now smeared, and her hair was knotted and greasy.

A knock at the door made her jump. She pulled the duvet over her head, hoping they would leave. A second knock caused her to raise her head from the pillow and look toward the door. A part of her was curious about who it might be. She and Roxy never had visitors. They didn't even have friends.

'Who is it?' she called out in a strained voice.

'It's Lewis,' a muffled voice replied.

He was the last person she wanted to see right now. She was still feeling the comedown of the heroin, and no doubt he was bringing more bad news.

'Go away!' she shouted before plumping her head back down on the pillow and pulling the covers over her.

'Please open the door, Devlin,' Lewis shouted back. 'I need to speak to you. It's important.'

Devlin huffed. She slowly slipped out of bed and stumbled over to the front door. She felt a chill creep around her skin and shivered. As she pulled the door ajar, the security chain prevented it from opening any further. Lewis peered through the gap.

'What?' she asked with a tired sigh.

'Are you going to open the door and let me in?' Lewis replied.

She exhaled in frustration. Why was he making this so difficult? *If he wants to talk, just talk.* She took the chain off and opened the door fully. She stepped aside, allowing Lewis to enter.

'So?' she said, eager for him to get on with it.

'How are you doing? Are you sleeping?'

'Is that why you came? To ask me that?' she answered irritably.

'No, I came to tell you we have a lead on Roxy's murder.'

Suddenly, Devlin was wide awake and listening.

'You know who did it?'

'No, but we found a videotape of the murder.'

'A videotape? You mean they filmed it?'

Lewis nodded. Devlin felt sick. She walked over to the bed and sat down on the edge.

'If they filmed it, surely you know who killed her.'

Lewis sat down next to her. He desperately wanted to put his arm around her shoulder but knew it would be inappropriate. He was there on a professional basis, and he didn't want to cross a line.

'The killer is wearing a mask. I don't like to ask this of you, but would you be willing to watch it to see if there's anything about this man you recognise?'

Devlin looked up at him with a look of disgust on her face.

'I don't think so,' she said, shaking her head.

'I'm not asking you to watch the whole thing, but right now, it could be our only shot of finding her killer.'

Devlin had to think. She wanted the culprit to pay for what they did, but she didn't want to see Roxy moments before her death. How helpless and scared she must have been, but this could be the only way of finding justice.

#

Two hours later, Devlin found herself sitting in a quiet office of the police station staring at a television set. She was breathing heavily with nerves. She desperately wanted to rush out of the room, but she had to stay brave for Roxy. She had to help the police find this bastard. Her fingers were shaking as she played with the bracelet around her wrist. She tried to draw strength from it, to feel Roxy with her.

Lewis turned off the lights, plunging them into darkness. He sat down next to her and pressed play on a television remote. The glow of the screen lit up Devlin's face. Her eyes were transfixed on the static.

The grainy footage began. It depicted a small dark room with a bed in the centre. A six-foot tall topless man wearing a white plastic face mask with the eyes cut out guided Roxy into the shot. Devlin could see she was not in a lucid state. Her eyes were drowsy, and her body was flopping about. She had been stripped down to her underwear.

The muscular masked man sat Roxy down on the bed. As he turned his back toward the camera, part of a tattoo peering out from the top of his trousers could be seen. They looked like the tips of wings.

The tape jump-cut to several seconds later. The masked man pushed Roxy, and she swayed back and forth, no longer in control of her body. Then he slapped her four times across the face. The slaps got harder each time. Devlin screwed up her face in disgust. She clutched at the bracelet as his palm snapped against Roxy's cheek.

Devlin's heart was pounding inside her chest. She wasn't sure how much of this she could take. Her eyes shifted down to the masked man's hand, scrunching up into a fist. Devlin swore she could hear the sound of Roxy's nose breaking as his fist smashed into her face. Blood spurted onto the bed sheet, and Roxy fell back onto the bed. Devlin threw up a hand over her face, tears welling in her eyes.

An arm reached into the shot holding a large hunting knife. Pen markings on the extended arm caught her attention. They read "S1-T3, S2-T1, S3-T2". The masked man received the knife and moved toward Roxy with menace.

Devlin turned away.

'Turn it off,' she cried.

Lewis reacted quickly, pressing stop on the remote. The picture turned black. Devlin held her hands over her face breathing heavily. Lewis switched on the lights and crouched down before her.

'Was there anything you recognised? The way he moved, his mannerisms, the tattoo on his back? What about the markings on the arm?'

Devlin removed her hands to reveal tears streaming down her face.

'I don't know. Nothing was familiar. I can't do this anymore. I want to go home now.'

'Please, Devlin, think. If there is anything, you need to tell me.'

Devlin looked Lewis square in the eye, her brows furrowing. 'I don't know.'

Devlin jumped up from her seat and rushed out of the room. Lewis was about to chase her, but he thought it best to leave her. He felt bad for putting her through such distress, but he needed to do whatever it took to find the people who did this.

Devlin stood outside the police station breathing in the fresh air and calming herself down. She leaned up against a wall and replayed the tape in her head. She couldn't believe someone was capable of doing that to another person. Why did they kill her? What had she ever done to deserve that kind of treatment? As her breathing steadied, her sadness turned to anger, and she felt her fists clench.

#

The rain fell heavy on the headstones scattered about the graveyard. Devlin stood by a freshly filled in grave, dressed in black. She held an umbrella shielding her from the elements. Her mascara ran beneath her sad, tear-filled eyes as she stared down at the temporary cross planted in the soil, a plaque read "Roxanne Campbell, 1963 - 1988".

Devlin looked at the charm bracelet studying the individual charms dangling. She closed her eyes and took a deep breath.

'I remember what you told me.' Her eyes flicked open, staring daggers off into the distance. 'If I ever get the chance, I promise I will.'

CHAPTER 9

It was a bitingly cold night, with a light frost in the air. The window lights of the video rental store acted like a beacon in the middle of the darkness. Devlin approached the door and pushed only to find it locked. She peered through the glass for signs of life but found none. She knew Reese stuck around late after work; it was the best time to sell. She knocked loudly on the pane, hoping he heard.

Reese poked his head out from the back room and squinted to see who was disturbing him. He realised it was Devlin and headed over to the door, unlocking the many locks. He pulled it slightly ajar and stuck his head through the gap.

'We're closed,' he said.

'I need some more.'

Reese considered her request a brief moment and then nodded. He allowed Devlin to enter and then, before closing the door, gave a glance up and down the road to ensure no one was watching.

Reese led Devlin into the back room where a television set on a counter hooked up to several VHS recorders was playing a film. Each VCR was recording. He gave a cursory scan across each machine to check they were still acting as intended.

'I'm surprised to see you back so soon. I guess you've got lost time to catch up on,' Reese said as he made his way over to a desk and pulled open the bottom drawer. Devlin was standing by the VCRs casting a curious eye over them. Reese caught her from the corner of his eye as he took a tin out of the drawer.

'Don't touch that. I'm making bootleg copies. A little money on the side,' he said with a cheeky grin.

Devlin turned to the television screen to see what film he was duplicating. Judging by the grainy quality and cheap camera work, it wasn't anything from Hollywood. Then suddenly, someone appeared in the shot that took her breath away. It was the masked man, the one that killed Roxy. Devlin's eyes locked onto him. She pushed her face forward for a clearer look and to be sure her mind wasn't playing tricks on her. The white mask was no doubt the same, but could it be the same man? Then it was confirmed as he turned his back toward the camera, the same hint of a tattoo peaking out from the top of his trousers.

Devlin's breathing intensified. She was half expecting him to murder another girl in front of her, but instead, the woman he was with was consenting to his advances, and she was giving as good as she got.

'Who is that?' Devlin said to Reese as he weighed up white powder into a small plastic bag.

'I have no idea,' he replied. 'The VHS case is just by you.'

Devlin found the case perched precariously on the counter and picked it up. The title of the film was *Fetish Funhouse*. No other details were given. No plot synopsis—what a surprise!—and no cast list either. The only marking was on the other side of the cover. Next to a picture of a half-naked woman was the name "Hardwood Films".

'You want to buy a copy?' Reese said, sealing up the plastic bag.

Devlin put the case down and rushed for the door.

'Hey!' Reese called out.

Devlin stopped and looked back at him. He was waving the small bag of powder in the air. Devlin reached out and snatched it from his hand. She took a wad of cash from her handbag and slapped it into his open palm.

'Thank you,' he said as she disappeared through the door.

#

Devlin sat on the floor of the apartment in front of a large dresser. It contained a multitude of clothes Roxy had collected over the years for work. Some clients had pretty strict ideas about what they wanted her to wear, and so she had to cater for various occasions and fetishes.

Devlin slid open the bottom drawer and rummaged through the unkempt apparel. She tugged at a T-shirt caught under a bundle and caught a whiff of its smell. She held it up to her nose and drew in a deep breath. It was Roxy's scent. She felt her heart skip a beat. It felt like she was in the room with her.

She placed the T-shirt gently to one side and continued her search. She found what she was looking for, a blonde wig. She held it up with her hand inside the cap allowing the hair to drape, and then combed it with her fingers.

CHAPTER 10

Hardwood Films was based in a small Victorian-era warehouse in the Soho area of London. Devlin stared up at the large imposing building, the blonde wig helping change her appearance. On the outside, it was hard to tell if there was a film studio inside, but Devlin had confirmed the address with a page torn from the Yellow Pages. She assumed the camouflage on the outside was intentional. The public could remain unaware of what goes on inside if they were even curious in the first place.

She headed toward a set of large gate-like doors tucked down in the corner of the building and stepped cautiously inside via an open smaller door housed within one of the gates.

The large open space was rigged with lighting in the ceiling shining down on a double bed surrounded by three false walls giving the impression of a bedroom. To one side was a small office with windows facing out onto the set. On the opposite side were doors leading off to a dressing room and an editing/storage room.

Devlin stood in the darkness watching the cast and crew walk about busy. She studied each one carefully, marking them down in her head as potential suspects.

A tall slim man was crouched, fiddling with nobs and dials on a sound recorder. He wore a set of headphones over his dark permed hair. He glanced over at Devlin, giving her a grin and wink. She made a mental note of his face and turned away to the next target.

A slightly rotund man sporting a ponytail and wearing thin, wiry glasses was wiping the lens of his camera cradled securely on a tripod. He scratched at his ear, where a ballpoint pen was wedged.

Target number three sat on the floor by the bed in a dressing gown, repeating a series of crunches. With his chiselled features and toned body peeking through the gap in his gown, Devlin suspected he was one of the actors. His slicked-back dark hair and clean-shaven face resembled a catalogue model.

Devlin's attention was drawn to two young girls exiting the dressing room wearing silk gowns and deep in conversation with each other. Both tall and blonde, they were stereotypical for this industry; smooth skin, slim bodies and large breasts. Like a couple of twins, though one of them was more doe-eyed than the other. Devlin was beginning to get a clear picture of this world, which wasn't much different from her own. Maybe she would blend in here after all.

A young girl with kind eyes and a sweet smile approached Devlin. She was tying her strawberry blonde hair up in a ponytail.

'Hey. Are you okay? You look a little lost,' she said with an American accent.

'I'd like to apply for a job,' Devlin replied.

'Oh, okay. You'd need to speak to Patrick. He owns the studio. I think he's in his office. Come with me.'

She approached the office door and gently knocked. Devlin stared through the glass windows at a tall, handsome man with a groomed beard and combed-back black hair. He was talking irately on the telephone, pacing up and down the room. He took notice of the girl's presence and beckoned her in. He screamed something Devlin couldn't quite hear into the phone and slammed the receiver down.

A few words were exchanged with the American girl, and then Devlin felt her heart rate increase as he looked through the window at her. His piercing brown eyes stared into her soul, judging her.

'Go right in. He's keen to meet you,' the yank said to Devlin.

Devlin cautiously neared the door and stepped into the office.

'Please, take a seat,' Patrick said with a warm smile.

Devlin perched herself on the edge of a wooden chair on the other side of his large hardwood desk. He sat in a comfortable-looking leather office chair and gave her a lengthy glare before speaking.

'So, first things first. What's your name?'

'Rose.'

'Rose,' he repeated, making a note on a pad. He glanced up at her expecting more, pen at the ready.

'Do you have a last name, Rose?' he said.

Devlin was about to speak but then paused. She needed a fake surname, something she hadn't considered when planning her first name. She took a moment glancing down at the charm bracelet, and then gave him an answer.

'Charm. Rose Charm,' she replied confidently.

'Rose Charm,' Patrick said, writing it down. 'I like that. Have you done any films before?'

Devlin shook her head. He stared at her with raised eyebrows.

'Oh, I was going to say you seemed familiar. I thought maybe I'd seen you in something. You must just have one of those faces.'

'I get that a lot.'

'I'm sure you do. Anyway, what are your limits?'

'What do you mean?' she said with a frown of confusion.

'Is there anything you're not willing to do on camera? Oral, anal etc.'

Any other woman would have been stunned right now, but Devlin was used to this kind of talk by men, so she didn't even flinch.

'I'll do anything,' she said with an air of arrogance.

Patrick seemed to like that answer as he received it with a wry smile and a slight nod of his head.

'Fantastic. Okay, if you could just stand up and remove your clothes.'

Devlin hesitated. 'Excuse me?'

'I need to see you naked. It's kind of important. I have to ensure you have no horrible scars or defects. I don't want that kind of shit in my films. If you're not comfortable with that, then I suggest you leave. This business isn't for you.'

Devlin glanced over her shoulders at the large windows behind her, looking at the set filled with people.

'Don't expect me to close the blinds,' he said. 'If you can't be naked in front of them, you're gonna have a hard time working here.'

Devlin took a deep breath and thought of Roxy. She slowly stood and began peeling away each piece of clothing. First, her jacket, then her dress, followed by her underwear. Patrick watched intently until she stood before him, fully undressed. She could sense eyes on the other side of the windows and felt her face turn red. Patrick stood up and walked around the desk. She tried to look anywhere except directly at him as he skulked around her, analysing every inch of her body. He reached out and brushed fingers delicately across her lower back, and she shivered.

'Very nice. Okay, you can put your clothes back on,' he said.

Devlin hastily picked up her garments and covered herself again. Patrick made his way back over to his chair behind the desk.

'I'll be honest. I'm not looking for any new talent right now, so I can't give you a permanent contract, but there's something about you that I think could get an audience, and I don't want to risk losing that. We're halfway through shooting a new film, and

I think I have an idea for a scene you'd be perfect for. Pay is
£500 per scene. Because you're untested, we'll start you on a
probationary period. During this time, you'll only get paid if we
decide to use the scene. That may seem unfair, but every studio
in the country works that way. Does that sound okay to you?'

Devlin nodded.

'Good. We're short on time, so I'd like to get the scene shot
tomorrow. Okay?'

Devlin gave another nod. She wanted to wrap this up as
quickly as possible.

'Excellent,' Patrick said as he reached into a drawer and
pulled out a document placing it on the desk in front of Devlin.

'I need you to sign this agreement. It's standard boilerplate
stuff to protect the studio.'

Devlin did not hesitate to pick up a pen and scribble her
signature.

'And also a photo for my records.'

Patrick whipped out a polaroid camera and snapped a quick
shot of Devlin's face, the flash blinding her. He yanked the
ejected photo out of its dispenser and placed it to one side.

Patrick snatched the document back and returned it to the
drawer. Just as Devlin thought the meeting was over, the door
burst open, making her jump, and the catalogue model in the
dressing gown strolled into the room.

'Patrick! Are we going to shoot today or what?' he said,
frustrated.

'I'll be right out. Oh, Ricky, I'd like you to meet Rose Charm.
A temporary addition to our team with the potential to extend
her stay.' He winked at Devlin. 'She'll be shooting a scene with
you tomorrow.'

Ricky towered over Devlin, staring down at her. She looked
up at him nervously, his bulging muscles protruding through the
thin cloth of his gown. He grinned, revealing perky white teeth.

'Hello,' he said, taking Devlin's hand and kissing it like a lothario. 'I'm Ricky Romero. I look forward to working together. Perhaps you'd like to join us tonight at the Dream Lounge. I'll have a private booth, and we can get to know each other first.'

Devlin forced a smile and gently pulled her hand from his grip.

'Get yourself ready, Ricky. I'm on my way now,' Patrick ordered as he stood.

'I was born ready,' Ricky replied obnoxiously. He gave Devlin a wink and then stepped out of the office.

Patrick extended a hand to Devlin, and she stood to shake it.

'We'll see you tomorrow at 9 a.m.'

Devlin wasted no time walking at a hurried pace out of the office. She passed through the busy studio, making a beeline for the door. She gave one last glance over her shoulder to see Ricky slipping off his robe, letting it drop to the floor, exposing his naked body. He turned around to reveal a tattoo on his lower back, forcing Devlin to halt and stare. She thought back to the tattoo of the masked man and was sure it was the same. It was him; it had to be him. What were the odds of him having the same tattoo in the same location on his body? Now she just needed a plan of action.

She noticed a toolbox near her, the handle of a hammer protruding out. She reached down, making sure no one was watching, and took the hammer secreting it in her handbag. Nobody saw her. They were two busy prepping the shot as Ricky climbed onto the bed with the two blondes. Devlin turned and left the studio, her mind on murder.

CHAPTER 11

The Dream Lounge was one of the most popular nightclubs in the city. It was the place everyone wanted to party, although it wasn't always easy to get in. Wealth and fame were the guaranteed ticket, but attractive women had no problem persuading the bouncers to step aside.

Devlin used this to her advantage, gaining entry to the bustling room. Deafening dance music played to a gyrating and bouncing crowd, and bright, colourful lights darted around the darkness.

Devlin blended in amongst them, scanning the VIP booths around the edge of the dance floor, looking for her target.

There he was, sitting between the two blonde actresses he had been "acting" with only a few hours earlier. Ricky leaned forward toward a glass table and snorted a line of cocaine from the surface with a rolled-up bank note. He lifted his head to reveal wide eyes taking in the atmosphere. He then wiped the remaining powder from his nose and took a large gulp of his vodka and coke.

Devlin pushed her way through the herd to get closer to Ricky and expose herself to him on the dance floor. She began dancing along to *I'll Be Good* by Rene & Angela. It didn't take long for him to notice her as she wiggled her slender body, caressing her hips with her soft hands. She could see in his eyes she had his attention. He extended a finger and beckoned her toward him. Devlin forced a smile and made her way up a series of steps toward his booth.

Ricky maintained his focus on Devlin as he spoke to the two women alongside him.

'Stephanie, Chantelle, get out of here,' he said.

'What?' Chantelle replied. She was the head of the double act as Stephanie was already about to follow orders and stand when Chantelle grabbed her wrist, pulling her back down.

'I said scram. Go,' Ricky reiterated.

'Why?' Chantelle asked, her brows furrowed.

Ricky grabbed Chantelle by the throat and pushed his face close to her.

'Because I'm sick of looking at you,' he said through gritted teeth. 'Now do as you're told and fuck off!'

Ricky released his grip, pushing her back against the padded backboard of the seating. Stephanie watched on in horror. Devlin paused to see how this would play out.

Chantelle jumped up from her seat on the verge of tears. She pushed past Devlin and disappeared into the crowd of dancers, followed by a worried Stephanie.

Ricky seductively rubbed the velour cushion next to him, inviting Devlin to sit. She did, but not close enough, forcing Ricky to slide along the bench and rub his body against hers, throwing an arm over her shoulder.

'You're the new girl. Rose, wasn't it?' he said, turning on the charm.

'That's right.'

'Patrick has struck gold with you, if you don't mind me saying.'

Devlin acted coy. She wanted Ricky to think he was in control and domineering. He caught her glance down at the cocaine piled on the glass table and gestured toward it.

'Be my guest,' he said.

Devlin had never taken cocaine before but was well aware of its effects. She knew what she was about to do, but a part of her was worried she wouldn't be able to go through with it when the time came. Perhaps one sniff would give her the extra confidence she needed. She leant forward and snorted the line. It rushed up her nostril and burned like fire, and immediately, she felt the rush. Her heart rate increased, and she felt more alive than she ever had before.

'Good?' Ricky asked.

Devlin gave an erratic nod causing Ricky to grin.

'You're a very beautiful woman.'

'Stop it, you're embarrassing me,' Devlin replied playfully.

Ricky placed a hand on Devlin's thigh and rubbed it up and down, feeling her soft skin. She looked into his eyes.

'You know, I think you're really handsome. I'm excited about our scene together tomorrow,' she said.

'So am I.'

'In fact, I was wondering if we could rehearse.'

Ricky was taken aback by her forwardness. At first sight, this girl didn't seem the promiscuous type. He was certain he would have to work hard to get her anywhere near his bedroom tonight. Now she was giving it to him on a platter.

'You don't mess around, do you?'

Devlin shook her head.

'Well then,' Ricky said. 'why don't we head back to my place, and we can try a few things?'

'I'd love to,' Devlin replied, giving him a devilish grin.

They made the short journey back to Ricky's apartment in his bright red Porsche 911. He revved the engine, trying to impress her, and she feigned arousal giving him the reaction he was hoping for.

#

Devlin and Ricky entered the lavish apartment. It was the epitome of stylish 80s decor. Bright white walls with pastel-coloured furniture that looked more like sculptures. Artwork of nude women and posters of adult films starring Ricky Romero dotted around. Devlin placed her handbag on the sofa as Ricky made his way over to the kitchen.

'Can I get you a drink?' he called out before disappearing through a door.

'Please,' Devlin called out.

While he was preoccupied, Devlin studied the habitat of the man she was about to kill to get a clearer picture of him. There was very little in the way of books or records, but many photo albums were lined up on a shelf. She selected one randomly and flipped it open to reveal pictures of Ricky naked in various poses. He had a high opinion of himself. Vanity and arrogance wouldn't begin to cover it. She heard Ricky coming back and hastily put the album back.

He reappeared from the kitchen carrying two glasses of red wine.

'This is such a nice place. You must be very rich,' Devlin said, taking the glass he handed to her.

'I do all right for myself. Cheers.'

They clinked glasses, and both took a sip.

'Take a seat,' he said, gesturing toward the sofa.

Devlin sat on the white leather sofa, placing her wine on an oddly shaped coffee table in front of her. Ricky placed himself next to her, throwing his arm over the back of the sofa.

'How long have you been making films?' she asked.

'Come on, let's not talk shop. This is strictly pleasure,' he replied, looking deep into Devlin's eyes, becoming lost in their bright blue colour. 'You have such beautiful eyes.'

'You don't need to flatter me. We both know what's about to happen.'

Devlin leant forward, and they kissed passionately. Ricky cupped her breast in his large hand and squeezed. She pushed his hand away.

'Not here. Go and make yourself comfortable in the bedroom. I have a surprise for you,' she whispered.

'I like surprises,' he replied excitedly.

'Then you'll love this one. Bathroom?'

Ricky pointed over to a door on the other side of the room.

Devlin stood and collected her handbag. He watched her rear, his mouth watering as her hips wiggled. She glanced over her shoulder at him, winking before entering the bathroom.

Ricky rushed into the bedroom, almost tripping over. He sat on the edge of the bed and collected a mirror from the bedside table prepared with a line of cocaine. He snorted it and began tearing his clothes off like a randy teenager.

Devlin stepped out of the bathroom. She had removed her leather jacket and dress and paced across the living room wearing only lingerie with stockings and suspenders. She caught a glimpse of herself in a mirror and took a deep breath. *This was it*, she thought. *Stay strong*.

Devlin found Ricky lounging on the bed, his tight underwear doing a poor job of concealing his modesty.

'What do you think?' she asked, twirling so he could see every inch of her.

Ricky sat up against the headboard to get a clearer view of the half-dressed body teasing him.

He grinned. 'Very nice.'

Devlin placed her handbag down on the floor by the bed. She whipped a couple of suit ties off the wardrobe door handle, holding them up.

'How about a little bondage?' she asked.

'Now you're talking,' he replied, barely able to contain his excitement.

As Devlin neared him, she caught sight of the lines of cocaine sitting on the mirror beside the bed. She could do with another hit. Her heart was in her mouth, and she needed something to help her power through. She bent over, ensuring her bottom stuck up in the air. As she snorted a line, Ricky's eyes were transfixed on her rear. He extended a hand to caress it, but she quickly turned, slapping his hand away.

'All in good time,' she said.

Devlin placed a hand on his hairy chest and pushed him back down onto the bed, straddling his body. She bound his wrists to the headboard and checked they were as tight as possible. She couldn't risk him breaking free. Devlin kissed him, feeling disgusted, but she needed him vulnerable and off-guard.

'Close your eyes,' she said, stroking his lids with soft fingers.

Ricky did as he was told. He enjoyed being bossed about for once. Most of the time, it was he who had to take control, but now he could just relax and enjoy it. Devlin made her way down his chest with kisses.

'You're good,' he said.

'It gets better.'

Devlin reached down the side of the bed and into her handbag. She pulled out the hammer. She liked its weight in her hand, the power it contained.

'How could it get better?' he asked.

'With you dead,' she replied, venom in her voice.

Ricky opened his eyes to find the hammer raised high above his head, the metal glistening in the dim light and Devlin looking down at him with fury.

'No!' he cried, trying to pull at his binds.

Devlin brought the hammer down hard, smashing into Ricky's face. His nose broke immediately, caving into the cavity of his skull. Devlin proceeded to raise the hammer and bring it down four more times until there was nothing recognisable about him. The amount of blood was immense, redecorating the walls and drenching Devlin's hands and face. Bits of bone and flesh scattered like jetsam.

Exhausted, she stared at the mess before her, hands shaking, breathing heavy. Her grip on the tool released, letting it drop to the floor with a soft thud. She climbed off his corpse and took a packet of cigarettes from her handbag, struggling to light one with nerve-shredded fingers. She made her way over to the window.

#

Devlin burst into her apartment, still shaking. She dumped her handbag on the floor and tossed the blonde wig to one side. She needed a fix. She needed to slow her heart and calm her nerves. Flashes of his face breaking were haunting her, and she needed to escape it. She opened the bedside drawer and removed a blue and red pencil case.

She sat down at the dining table and prepared a syringe. Pulling a belt tight around her arm, she penetrated her skin with the needle and injected the drug. She released the belt and relaxed in the chair. It felt good, but at the same time, guilt came over her.

She remembered how Roxy had been the one to get her off this drug, to get her clean and sober. They were long, drawn-out days of going cold turkey. Waking in the middle of the night, sweating and panting about the bed.

Roxy was always prepared with a cool flannel placing it on Devlin's forehead and stroking her hair to calm her.

'I can't take it anymore,' Devlin would say. 'I need a fix.'

'No, you don't,' Roxy would tell her.

Devlin tried to climb out of bed with the intention of going out and scoring a hit, but Roxy held her back and embraced her tightly.

'You don't need that poison. You will get through this.'

Eventually, Devlin would give in and start crying, Roxy rocking her gently like a child, telling her it would all be okay. Only then would Devlin be able to sleep again.

And now Roxy was gone, and Devlin was back where she started, back where she didn't want to be, and it was all because of those bastards. They took Roxy's life, and her's along with it.

One down, one to go.

CHAPTER 12

Another morning arrived and another day, waking to find the bed next to her empty. The space was looming larger every day, like the hole in her heart.

She extended her arm and stroked the bed, the charm bracelet jingling on her wrist. She hadn't taken it off since Lewis gave it to her. But something about it was different. She sat up and took a closer look. There was a broken link and a charm missing. She searched the duvet and under the pillows, but it was not to be found.

She jumped from the bed and rushed around the apartment, checking the carpet for any sign of it, but it was nowhere. A sinking feeling came over her. Did it fall off back at Ricky's place? She hoped to God it didn't.

#

She was too late. She planned to get there before anyone found Ricky's body, but police cars and officers were already swarming the building. There was no chance of her getting inside now. One of the officers caught her staring and was about to approach until Devlin turned away and quickened her pace.

She wasn't sure what to do. There was a chance it hadn't fallen off there, so sneaking in and getting caught wasn't worth the risk. How likely were they to connect it to her anyway if they did find the charm? He must have had thousands of women back at his place, and charm bracelets were not exactly rare. But it was Roxy's bracelet, and she felt by losing it, she was losing Roxy's memory.

She decided she had to let it go and hoped it turned up somewhere else.

#

Grantham stared down at Lewis asleep on his desk, snoring loudly. It was not unusual to find fellow detectives having spent the night at the station, but this was the first time Lewis had done it. Grantham held two mugs of coffee in his hands, a file tucked under one arm. He placed one mug down hard on the desk by Lewis's head, and he jumped awake.

He looked up at Grantham with tired eyes, his hair a mess and a piece of paper stuck to his cheek.

'Have you not been home?' Grantham said.

'No,' Lewis replied, pulling the paper from his face.

'You look like shit.'

Lewis looked at the dark coffee steaming in the mug.

'A cup of coffee, and I'll be fine,' he said, picking up the mug and taking a sip. It burned his tongue, but that only helped wake his senses.

'This might perk you up,' Grantham said, pulling the file from under his arm and placing it down on Lewis's desk.

Lewis took another sip of his coffee as he flipped open the cover. Grantham perched himself on the edge of his desk.

'In case your eyes are too tired to read right now,' Grantham said. 'A gentleman was found murdered in his home this morning. Ricky Romero, a well-known adult film actor.'

Lewis studied the case file curiously but couldn't see the point.

'Why are you telling me this?'

'Take a look at the pictures of the body.'

Lewis turned over pages to get to the crime scene photos. He screwed his face up in disgust. He could barcly see the body for the amount of blood there was. He shook his head, still oblivious to Grantham's reasoning, until he reached a photo of Ricky's wings tattoo. He paused and held the photograph up for a better look in the light.

'Seem familiar?' Grantham asked, waiting for the penny to drop.

'He's the masked man?'

'Looks that way. Turns out Romero has a record as well. Several instances of actual bodily harm against women.'

'Shit,' Lewis said, leaning back in his chair. 'So, who killed him?'

'Who the fuck knows? Not our case. What is our concern, however, is he didn't act alone. We know there was someone else in that room, and more than likely, he did it with someone he would have trusted. He is—or was—a regular performer for Hardwood Films. Might be worth starting there.'

'There's something else I stumbled upon last night.'

Lewis stood up and turned on a television set in the corner of the room. He pressed play on a remote, and the snuff film began playing on the screen.

'How many times have you watched this?' Grantham asked with concern.

'Too many times,' Lewis replied, slightly embarrassed. 'Take a look at this.'

Grantham stepped closer to the screen. Lewis paused the tape and pointed. In the corner of the room, a blurry shadow of what looked like a human figure could be seen in the background.

'Here, I noticed a person's shadow moving,' Lewis said.

'Well, that's just the cameraman's shadow, right?'

'No.' Lewis shook his head. 'Watch.'

He pressed play on the remote. Grantham watched as the shadow moved away, disappearing.

'The shadow leaves before the cameraman passes the knife. So it can't be their shadow. There was a third person in that room.'

Grantham nodded in agreement. 'Let's get to that film studio then.'

CHAPTER 13

Hardwood Films was silent for the first time in a long time. Devlin entered the quiet room finding Chantelle and Stephanie sitting on the bed crying, trying to comfort each other. No doubt they had heard the news about Ricky's death, though she couldn't understand why they would be so upset after the way he treated them last night. She thought they would be happy.

She couldn't concern herself too much with them, however. She had a job to do, and someone else here was responsible for Roxy's death.

'Hey,' a kind American voice said behind her.

Devlin turned to find the American girl smiling sweetly.

'Is this yours?' she asked, holding out her hand.

Sitting in the palm was the missing charm. Devlin's eyes lit up. She felt like a weight had been lifted off her.

'Yes,' Devlin said with delight. 'Thank you so much.'

She took the charm and studied it with relief. She didn't have to worry about the police finding it, and she could keep Roxy's memory intact.

'You're welcome. I found it on the floor yesterday. I noticed you had a charm bracelet and so kept it safe for when I saw you next.'

'I can't thank you enough. You don't know how much this bracelet means to me.'

Devlin clipped the charm back onto the bracelet and smiled.

'I'm Josie.'

Josie held out a hand to shake.

Devlin shook it.

'Rose.'

'So, did you hear what happened to Ricky last night?' Josie asked.

'Uh, no. I didn't,' Devlin lied.

'Someone murdered him. Can you believe that? If you ask me, I think it was one of the girls.'

'Why do you say that?'

'He always treated us like shit.' Josie glanced over at Chantelle and Stephanie, still in each other's embrace. 'Well, most of the time.'

Devlin looked over at them. Chantelle caught Devlin staring and shot daggers back at her through tear-filled eyes. Devlin turned away.

'If you ask me, I'm glad he's dead. The guy was a piece of shit. I heard he once beat a woman almost to death because she looked at him wrong,' Josie said.

'Rose,' Patrick called out from his office.

'The bossman calls,' Josie said before walking away.

Devlin approached a distraught Patrick. He reached out his hands and placed them on Devlin's shoulders.

'Thank you for coming in today, but I don't know if you heard the terrible news. Ricky was killed last night. Suffice it to say we won't be filming your scene today. However, I want to assure you the scene will be shot. I just need to make a few calls and find another actor. I'll be in touch.'

The phone in Patrick's office started ringing.

'Excuse me,' he said, entering the office and closing the door behind him.

Devlin was hoping to eliminate a few possible suspects today, but now it would look too suspicious if she hung around the studio when she was not needed. She headed toward the door and accidentally bumped into the cameraman.

'Oh, I'm so sorry,' he said with fear.

'Don't be. My fault,' she replied.

Devlin paused as she caught a glimpse of his bare arms. Written along the lower left arm were letters and numbers "S-3, T-2". She thought about the snuff film and the arm extending into the shot. They were the same type of markings, letters followed by numbers. Scene numbers and take numbers, she assumed.

Devlin studied the cameraman with interest as he cut through the studio toward the editing room on the other side. She took a deep breath clutching the bracelet in her hand, and followed him.

The cameraman stood at a shelf sorting through video tapes. Devlin appeared at the doorway, leaning up against the frame.

'Hi there,' she said.

The cameraman turned to her, startled.

'What do you want?' he said nervously.

'I just wanted to talk,' Devlin said as she slinked up toward him.

'About what?'

'I'm Rose. What's your name?'

'J-J-Jordan.'

Jordan pushed himself up against the shelf as Devlin came within inches of him. He didn't like his personal space being invaded, and he could feel panic setting in. She picked at a button on his shirt, and that only made matters worse.

'I like that name. It's a strong name. I bet you're really strong.'

Jordan was frozen, trying not to look down at Devlin. She ran her hand up his arm and caressed his poor excuse for muscles. In his head, he was praying for her to stop.

'Mmm, very nice,' she whispered.

Jordan pushed himself further back against the shelf. Videotapes toppled onto the floor.

'So you're the cameraman?' Devlin asked.

'Y-Y-Yeah.'

'I bet you see some interesting things through that lens.'

'Sometimes,' Jordan struggled to say through panting breath.

'I'd like to hear about them.'

'I have to get back to work.'

Jordan tried to slip past Devlin, but she threw out an arm on either side of him, grabbing onto the shelf to keep him trapped.

'Oh, but I thought we could spend some time together,' she said with mock disappointment.

'Patrick doesn't like us socialising with the talent. He got very angry last time.'

Jordan was beginning to sweat. He could feel the beads running down his face.

'He doesn't have to know. What he doesn't know can't upset him, right? If you're frightened of getting caught here, why don't we meet somewhere else? I could come by your place tonight.'

'I can't. I'll be here working late. Besides, if he finds out, I'll be in big trouble,' Jordan replied.

'Oh, come on.'

Devlin stroked the side of his head, reaching around and playing with his ponytail. Jordan took his chance now that her arm was no longer containing him and pushed past her. Devlin almost tripped over backwards.

'I have to go before Patrick catches us,' Jordan said as he dashed out of the room.

Devlin gave an exhale of frustration. She thought he would be easy, but he's proving more difficult than Ricky. She needed to try a new tactic.

She was about to exit the editing room when she caught sight of Lewis entering the studio alongside Grantham. She froze. As Lewis scanned the room, he spotted Devlin and frowned. She quickly turned away, hiding her face hoping he hadn't recognised her. Surely the wig would be enough from a distance.

Lewis frowned and was about to walk over to her.

'Lewis,' Grantham said, gesturing for him to follow.

Lewis ignored the girl in the editing room and obeyed his superior. He was probably mistaken anyway.

Devlin stood by the side of the door and peered out, watching Lewis and Grantham approach the door of Patrick's office and knock.

Devlin slipped out of the room and walked at a quick pace through the studio toward the main entrance keeping her face covered. Chantelle watched her from the bed, still wiping away tears. She stood up and pursued Devlin.

#

When Devlin stepped outside, she breathed a sigh of relief. That was too close. If Lewis had seen her, it would have blown her whole plan. She needed to be a lot more cautious. Now that Ricky was dead, no doubt the police would be sniffing around the studio.

'Hey, you. New girl,' Devlin heard over her shoulder.

She turned to see Chantelle approaching her with menace.

'I saw you last night, leaving the club with Ricky!' Chantelle shouted.

'So?'

'So, I think you killed him.'

Chantelle had now pushed her face into Devlin's in a threatening manner. Devlin tried to stay calm.

'I don't know what you're talking about,' Devlin said, trying to turn, but Chantelle grabbed her arm, pulling her back.

'I don't know why Patrick hired you. You're a terrible actress.'

'You're crazy,' Devlin replied, shaking her head.

Chantelle pulled her in close and looked deep into her eyes.

'I don't know who you are or what you're doing, but I know you killed Ricky, and when I find the evidence you did, I'm going straight to the police,' Chantelle seethed.

'Leave me alone,' Devlin said, pulling her arm from Chantelle's grip and turning to walk away.

'Watch your back, new girl,' Chantelle called out to her.

CHAPTER 14

Patrick leant back in his chair and stared at Lewis and Grantham sat before him. He was not unused to the police visiting him. The porn industry still had its enemies, and they liked to make delusional claims about the kind of entertainment they were making. The police, having to follow up on these accusations, always arrived a little irritated by their need to investigate, knowing full well nothing illegal was being done. He was relaxed around their presence, and today was no different. After all, with Ricky's death, he was expecting them.

'I assume you're here regarding the death of Ricky Romero. I was shocked to hear of his death, but I can't say I was all too surprised,' Patrick said.

'How come?' Grantham asked curiously.

'Ricky knew how to upset people. Over the years, he's made a lot of enemies. Women he screwed over, angry husbands. The list is endless. You'll have your work cut out for you with this one.'

'Thank you for the warning,' Lewis said, 'but I'm afraid we're not here to investigate the death of Mr Romero. Our colleagues will be dealing with that case.'

'I see. Then why are you here? More complaints from the neighbours?'

'We're investigating the death of Roxanne Campbell,' Lewis said.

'Who?'

Lewis took out a photograph of Roxy from his inside pocket and passed it over to Patrick. He sat forward to look at it. It was a police mugshot. Looking into the case, Lewis had discovered Roxy's criminal record. She'd had her fair share of run-ins with the police over the years.

'Do you recognise her?' Lewis asked.

'I've never seen this girl before,' Patrick replied, passing the photograph back to Lewis.

Grantham reached into a nearby briefcase and took out the VHS tape labelled with the red "X" in an evidence bag. He placed it down on the desk in front of Patrick.

'How about this tape?' Grantham asked. 'Seem familiar?'

Patrick picked up the bag and studied the tape inside. He shook his head.

'What exactly are you getting at here?' he asked them.

'That tape depicts the murder of Roxanne Campbell by a masked man. We believe that man to be Ricky Romero,' Lewis said.

'You can't be serious. Ricky, murdering a girl on this tape?'

Lewis replied with a simple nod.

'Wait a second. If the man was masked, how do you suspect it was Ricky?' Patrick asked with a smirk.

'Part of a tattoo can be seen on the man's lower back. It matches Mr Romero's,' Lewis answered confidently.

Patrick sat back in his chair, the leather creaking beneath him.

'Was Mr Romero exclusive to your studio?' Grantham asked.

Patrick was no longer relaxed. He knew what they were getting at, and he didn't like it. He sat forward, leaning in close to ensure they could hear him.

'If you're implying I made this tape, you're very much mistaken. Ricky was never exclusive to my films. He was freelance; he worked wherever the money was. He could have made this with anyone.'

'Well, you're the one in the industry. Anyone you can think of in particular?' Grantham asked, knowing full well he was pushing Patrick's buttons. There was something about this man he didn't like, and he wanted to test him.

'I don't know anyone that would be capable of something like this,' Patrick answered sternly.

'So, you've never considered the snuff genre yourself?' Grantham continued to push.

'I'm not even going to dignify that with an answer. I find the mere suggestion offensive. I'm a creator of entertainment. Murder is not entertainment.'

'It was entertainment to someone,' Lewis added.

Grantham's test of Patrick was complete, and for now, he'd passed. The man hadn't said a wrong word, but that was never proof of innocence. He would still be a potential suspect until he could be eliminated from enquiries.

'Thank you for your help, Mr Levesque,' Grantham said, getting to his feet and collecting the videotape.

Lewis stood, and Patrick followed suit.

'Do you mind if we have a look around?' Lewis asked.

'As a matter of fact, I do,' Patrick snapped back.

'Why's that?'

'This is an adult film studio. We have sensitive material here, and I have my rights. You come back with a search warrant, you can look wherever you like.'

'That kind of answer makes us suspicious,' Lewis said.

Grantham was proud of Lewis. They'd only been partners for a year, and already he was learning how to play with suspects and try to trip them up.

'I don't care.' Patrick scowled at them. 'I've got nothing to hide. Come back with a warrant.'

'We'll do that,' Lewis replied with a hint of a smile.

CHAPTER 15

The syringe drank the liquid as Devlin pulled the plunger back. A knock at the door made her jump, and she almost dropped the spoon.

'Who is it?' she called out.

'It's Lewis,' a voice on the other side replied.

Devlin put the syringe and spoon back inside the pencil case and took it over to the bedside table, slipping it inside a drawer. She took a quick look at herself in the mirror and tried to improve her appearance, adjusting her hair and rubbing her eyes before answering the door.

She smiled as Lewis entered.

'How are you doing?' he asked.

'I'm good. I'm coping,' she said, closing the door behind him.

'Good. I know it's late coming, but I wanted to apologise for making you watch the tape. I should never have asked you to. It wasn't right to put you through that.'

'It's okay. I know you were just doing what you thought you had to. Can I get you a drink?' she asked.

'No, I can't stay. I just wanted to stop by and give you an update on the investigation.'

'Oh, have you found something?'

'Are you familiar with the name Ricky Romero?'

Devlin's heart began pounding. She could feel her mouth go dry.

'No,' she said quietly.

'Roxy never mentioned him at all?'

'Never, why?'

'He was found murdered this morning. We believe he was the masked man in the tape.'

Lewis reached into his pocket and took out a picture of Ricky. It was a promotional advert for a film, cut from a magazine. He passed it to her.

'Do you recognise him?' he asked.

Devlin stared at the photo. The image of his face breaking like an egg passed through her mind. The blood sprayed up the walls, brains flying around the room. She passed the photo back to Lewis shaking her head.

'No. Who is he?'

'An adult film actor. I thought if Roxy knew him, it might explain their connection.'

Devlin took a seat at the dining table. Her legs felt like jelly, and she was worried she would collapse in front of Lewis.

'Who killed him?' Devlin asked.

'No idea,' Lewis replied, taking a seat next to her. 'Although the list of potential suspects is as long as my arm.'

Devlin was relieved to hear that. It would probably be a while before they even suspected her. She would surely have enough time to kill Jordan.

'Of course,' Lewis continued. 'we know he wasn't alone in the act of Roxy's murder, so we're still looking for others who were involved. It's entirely possible he couldn't be trusted to keep quiet, and his co-conspirators decided to silence him. That's just my theory right now, though. Anyway, I better be going.'

Lewis stood and made his way to the door. Devlin followed him. He stopped and turned to her.

'I hope you don't mind me saying, but I worry about you alone in this apartment.'

Devlin smiled. 'I appreciate your concern, but I'm fine.'

'You say that, but you look like you haven't eaten a proper meal in days.'

Devlin shrugged her shoulders. 'I'm not much of a cook,' she said.

'I know I'm going beyond my duties as an officer here, but how would you like to come to mine this evening and I cook you something?'

'Oh,' Devlin replied, taken aback.

Lewis looked away in embarrassment.

'Sorry. I shouldn't have —'

'It's okay. I'd love to,' she said.

Lewis smiled. 'Great. I'll come by and pick you up on my way home. About seven?'

'Seven is good.'

'Well, I'll see you later then.'

Lewis opened the door and gave her a quick smile before closing it behind him. Devlin grinned to herself. Suddenly, she didn't feel so alone anymore.

CHAPTER 16

Lewis's apartment was minimalist. There wasn't much on the walls, and only the necessary furniture; tables, chairs etc. Boxes of unpacked items were stacked around. It looked as though he had only just moved in despite living there for several months. That's the problem with a demanding job, very little time to live your life. Lewis would love a day to just switch off and put up some picture frames, but his police mind wouldn't allow it. He was always thinking about a case trying to find the next lead.

Devlin sat at a small dining table lit by candlelight. She had put on the classiest dress she could find in the apartment, which happened to be one of Roxy's. A little black number.

Lewis came from the kitchen carrying two plates of food. Steak and chips. The perfect balance of sophistication and simplicity. He placed one plate down in front of Devlin, and she admired the well-presented meal.

'I hope you like it. It's my own recipe.' Lewis smirked.

Lewis sat down opposite and laid a napkin over his lap. He eagerly picked up his knife and fork and began cutting into the medium-rare sirloin.

Devlin stared at the food, reluctant to eat. She appreciated the meal, but she wasn't actually hungry. All she could think about was another fix. The addiction had now consumed her again, and she could barely go an hour without a hit.

Lewis saw she wasn't eating and stopped chewing.

'Is something wrong?' he asked.

Devlin looked up at him.

'I'm sorry,' he said. 'I didn't even ask to see what you liked to eat. I can make you something else.' He was about to stand when Devlin's words stopped him.

'No, it's fine. This is perfect.'

Devlin smiled. She picked up the fork and stabbed a chip. She nibbled the end of it and forced a grin after swallowing.

Lewis felt relieved and continued eating.

#

Later that night, they sat on the sofa, each with a glass of wine, the soft, soothing melodies of Peter Gabriel's *In Your Eyes* playing in the background. Lewis collected a bottle from the coffee table and topped up Devlin's glass.

The last time she was in this situation, she killed someone, Devlin thought to herself. She had no intention of killing Lewis, though. She'd never met a man so kind and generous. He treated her like a person, not a performing doll like all her clients. Her faith in men was increasing.

Lewis topped up his glass before placing the bottle back on the coffee table.

'So, do you always invite grieving family and friends back to your place for dinner and wine?' she asked playfully.

'In my profession, it's the only way to meet people,' Lewis replied seriously.

Devlin was shocked. Had she got this man all wrong? Was he just like all the rest of them?

'Sorry, police humour.' Lewis smirked. 'Of course I don't.'

Devlin felt relief, taking a sip of her wine.

'What makes me so special?' She enquired curiously.

'You remind me of someone I used to know,' he said.

'Who?'

'Just an old friend. I guess I have a soft heart. I find it easy to care. I was worried about you. I just wanted to make sure you were okay. I know it can't be easy going through what you are,' he said.

'Well, I find ways to cope,' she said. 'But I appreciate your kindness. I don't think I've ever been treated like this by a man before.'

'Don't you ever think about giving it up? It's not exactly the safest job.'

'I didn't come here for a lecture on my profession. I don't need someone telling me how to live my life,' Devlin snapped back. Whenever anyone found out what she did for a living, they always tried to persuade her to give it up. They didn't understand that she was happy. It's not like someone was forcing her.

Lewis raised a defensive hand in surrender. 'I'm sorry, I didn't mean to judge. It's just, how do you get into something like that?'

'You just fall into it. I didn't have the best of childhoods. No father and a mother who drank. After running away from home and spending a few years homeless, I met Roxy. She saved my life. Taught me everything I know. At this point, I wouldn't know what else to do. Besides, the money is too good to turn down. Roxy used to say, "It's a man's world, and this is our way of levelling the playing field." She always had little sayings like that.'

Devlin froze, lost in thought. Thinking about Roxy was becoming harder each day. Her heart rate increased, and her sad eyes held back tears. Lewis could see Devlin's emotions rising and felt the need to say something to break the haunting silence.

'She must have really meant something to you,' he said.

Devlin broke free from her daydream and turned to him, smiling.

'More than you can imagine. Life's not the same without her.'

Lewis stared at Devlin, looking deeply into her eyes. They were a refreshing blue glistening in the dim light. He leaned forward to kiss her, but she backed away, pulling a face of shock.

'What are you doing?' she asked furiously.

'I'm sorry. I just thought—'

'Well, you thought wrong.'

Devlin slammed her glass down on the coffee table, spilling its contents on the hardwood surface. She jumped up from the sofa, rushing for the front door. Lewis put his glass down and chased after her.

'Devlin, please,' he called out.

Devlin grabbed her jacket from a coat hook and was about to open the door when Lewis grabbed her arm.

'Devlin.'

'Don't touch me,' she said, pulling her arm from his grip.

'I didn't mean to—'

'You know, I actually thought you were different, but you're just like every other guy. You're only after one thing!' she shouted.

'That's not true,' he pleaded.

'Just leave me alone.'

Devlin yanked open the front door and ran out, slamming it behind her. Lewis exhaled in frustration. He placed his hand on the door and banged his head up against it in shame.

Suddenly, Lewis felt the need to unpack one of those boxes. He flipped open the flaps and rummaged inside, finding an old, tatty shoebox. He sat down on the bed, taking off the lid to reveal a pile of letters and photographs. He stumbled upon a newspaper clipping with the headline "Prostitute Found Murdered" with a picture of an attractive young woman next to it. He stroked the image with his thumb. It still haunted him. Her name was Jenny. She had witnessed a brutal murder in Soho, but was refusing to speak for fear of her safety. Over the course of several weeks, Lewis would check in on her and try to persuade her to talk, offering promises to protect her. They became close, developing a connection to the point where he had gained her trust, and she was willing to sign a statement fingering the culprit. The man responsible was arrested, but two days later, Jenny turned up dead. Lewis had failed her, and the guilt hung around his neck like an albatross. He promised himself he would never let his personal feelings infringe on his professional career again, yet it seemed he couldn't help it. He wiped a tear away from his cheek and wondered how he could make things right with Devlin.

CHAPTER 17

The marijuana joint lit with ease, and sound-man Mike inhaled the fumes, holding them a moment in his lungs before breathing them out into Jordan's face.

'A friend brought this over from America. Some of the best gear I've ever had,' Mike said, passing the joint to Jordan, allowing him to take a drag and fill the editing room with more smoke. Jordan grinned.

'Good, huh?' Mike asked.

Jordan nodded with approval returning the joint to Mike.

'You want to buy some?'

'Definitely,' Jordan replied.

Mike held the joint between his lips and reached into his coat pocket. He took out a small bag of cannabis and handed it to Jordan. It was exchanged with cash, and Mike counted it to ensure it was the correct amount. He did trust Jordan, but sometimes the man was a little slow on the uptake and made mistakes.

Mike removed the joint from his lips and exhaled even more smoke, leaning back in his chair. The room was becoming cloudy.

'So, who do you think murdered Ricky?' Mike said, pontificating.

'I don't know,' Jordan said.

'I do,' Mike said.

Jordan sat forward curiously. 'Who?'

Mike leaned in close to Jordan's face. 'Patrick.'

'What? Why?'

'Got sick of his bullshit. He couldn't take it anymore and decided to bash his brains in.'

Jordan stared off into the distance with a look of worry on his face. Mike, realising Jordan wasn't catching on, burst out laughing.

'Wow, you are too easy. I'm just kidding,' he said forcefully.

Jordan forced a laugh, but he didn't find Mike funny. He was always teasing him, and he hated it.

'Patrick may be a huge arsehole,' Mike said, 'but I can't see him killing anyone. It was probably the pissed-off husband of some whore Ricky was fucking. That sounds more plausible. Either way, I can't say I'll miss the bastard,' he added before taking another drag.

Jordan nodded in agreement. That must have been who it was. At least he hoped that was the case.

'Right, let's get the fuck out of here,' Mike said, standing up.

'I can't,' Jordan said, disappointed.

'Why not?'

'Patrick wanted me to finish editing this scene before tomorrow.'

'Come on, it's eleven-thirty. You've done enough work for today. Besides, after a hit of this shit, your mind isn't going to be able to focus for a while,' Mike said with a grin, holding up the joint.

Jordan stood up. 'You know what? You're right,' he said, revelling in the rebellion. 'Are you up for going to the den?'

'Can't tonight. The missus is expecting me.'

'Well, I'm not going home yet. My mum will still be awake.'

'I can't believe you're forty and you still live with your mum,' Mike said, shaking his head.

'She needs me.'

Jordan picked up a ballpoint pen from the desk and cradled it on top of his ear. The two men grabbed their jackets off the back of each chair and headed for the door switching off the lights as they left.

Devlin watched as Jordan and Mike stepped out of the warehouse, pulling the door closed behind them and clipping on a padlock. She was hidden within a bush, a hood over her head. The dim light of a burning cigarette between her fingers.

The two men said their goodbyes and walked off in separate directions. Devlin tossed the cigarette and followed Jordan.

She stayed close behind him, desperate not to lose sight, but she didn't want to catch his attention either and walked as quietly as she could. After about five minutes, she tailed him into a dark alleyway and wondered where he was going.

She took cover behind a large commercial rubbish bin and witnessed Jordan approach the rear door to a small building. He knocked three times. The door swung open, and a large, heavy-set man stepped out. There was a brief exchange of words before the doorman allowed Jordan entry. The doorman then disappeared, closing the door behind him.

Devlin walked up to the door and scanned the building for any other sign of entry. She heard a commotion on the other side of the door and ducked to the side as it swung open. The doorman stormed out, holding another man by his shirt collar, almost carrying him. He released his grip, and the man collapsed to the wet ground.

'Get the hell out of here, you sick son of a bitch!' the doorman shouted.

While he was preoccupied, Devlin slipped through the door behind him. The doorman turned and re-entered, closing the door.

Devlin descended a metal spiral staircase and passed through a stone archway into a large open room. It was dimly lit, reflecting off the dampness on the brick walls.

The room was filled with thirty to forty men making their way around a set of tables set up at the edge of the room like market stalls. Each table contained VHS tapes and amateur photographs manned by a salesman showing off his wares. Some tables had a portable television set hooked up to a VCR, demonstrating the grainy quality of the films. Shocking images of rape and abuse were depicted on them. Devlin had to look away, memories of Roxy running through her mind.

Devlin caught sight of Jordan standing by a table browsing video tapes. She kept her eye on him while trying to blend in so as not to draw attention. She approached a table at random containing more VHS tapes. A crude sign made from cardboard read "Banned" in red ink. She lightly scanned the covers, moving over to the next table where other signs read "Hardcore" with subcategories such as "Straight", "Gay", and "Lesbian".

She came upon a sign that read "Kids" and felt sick to the pit of her stomach. The seedy-looking seller leaned forward and smiled with rotten teeth. He winked at her.

'See something you like?' he asked.

Devlin turned away in disgust, making her way over to another table. She found pirated copies of popular Hollywood films with crudely printed covers. No doubt these were provided by Reese's little operation.

She glanced over at Jordan again. He had finished browsing and was now heading around a corner out of sight. Devlin rushed after him and turned the corner just in time to see Jordan pass through a curtain being held open by a gaunt-looking man. As the curtain swung back into position, Devlin approached to go straight through, but the gaunt man stepped in her way.

'You want to watch, it's going to cost you. Hundred quid,' he said, with a whisper of a voice.

Through a gap in the curtain, Devlin could see Jordan enter a door to the side. She reached into her purse and pulled out a few notes. She slammed them into the man's hand and was about to push past, but he grabbed her wrist.

'If you're ever looking for work. I have a few positions open. I could make quite a penny from you,' the gaunt man said, taking Devlin's fake blonde hair in his fingers.

Devlin slapped his hand away and disappeared through the curtain.

'Enjoy the show,' he said, grinning.

The small booth was barely one metre by two metres, and Jordan could just about fit his wide frame in the swivel chair. In front of him was a box of tissues and a bottle of lotion. He stared through a glass window covered on the other side by a red curtain. He took his glasses off and cleaned them with a cloth before placing them back on his face.

The curtain automatically slid across to one side, revealing a small room with a single bed in the centre. A young girl of around fifteen years old sat on the bed in a silk robe, drugged and beaten. She looked around through heavy eyelids at the ring of mirrors circling her. All she could see was her sad reflection, not the perverse men behind them ogling her.

Jordan shifted in his seat to get comfortable and began unbuckling his belt. A knock at the door startled him.

'It's occupied!' he shouted as he glanced over his shoulder, irritated.

There was another knock.

'There's someone in here.'

Another knock.

Jordan re-buckled his belt and swivelled in the chair. He stood, opening the door and found Devlin standing before him, smiling, holding something behind her back.

'You? What are you doing here? How did you get in?' Jordan asked.

She placed a finger on his lips to silence him. She applied a little pressure, and he stepped back, falling into the chair behind him. Devlin closed the door, locking it. She stepped toward him, the corner of her mouth curling up.

'You shouldn't be here. We're not allowed to socialise with the talent,' he said nervously.

'Don't worry. Nobody will ever know. It's just you and me now.'

Jordan grinned. He realised there was no chance of him being caught here. He began unbuckling his belt again.

'I feel like I'm in heaven,' he said.

'Not yet,' she replied.

Devlin raised the hammer high above her. Jordan looked up at it in disbelief. She brought it down toward his head, but for a large man, his reactions were quick. He grabbed her wrist, holding the tool back from his skull, and then he threw up his other hand, grabbing her around the throat. He stood and pushed her back against the door, lifting her slightly from the floor. Devlin struggled to break free, but his grip was too tight.

'What are you doing?' he asked, terrified.

'You killed my friend,' Devlin strained her voice to say.

He bashed her wrist against the door, and she felt her hand weaken. The hammer slipped from her fingers, hitting the floor. He stared at her vengeful face with confusion.

'What are you talking about?' he asked.

Devlin was squirming, her elbows and heels knocking against the door. She needed to do something to get free. She saw the pen wedged on top of Jordan's ear and reached out with her free hand, yanking it from its cradle. She then plunged it deep into his neck, blood spraying out like a jet of water. His eyes widened in shock, gargling blood as he tried to speak. He released his grip on her, and she dropped down.

Jordan fell to one knee, pulling the pen from his neck, but that seemed to increase the blood flow now covering the floor. He placed a hand over the wound to stem the evacuation of life. Devlin picked up the hammer and looked down at him.

'You fucking bitch. Why?' he gurgled.

'You killed my friend. I know you were there. You filmed it,' she replied.

'Fuck you. I didn't do anything,' Jordan said, reaching out to grab her.

Devlin stepped back from his grasping hand and kicked him hard in the stomach. He wheezed in pain.

'You fucking whore,' he cried.

'Don't lie to me!'

Jordan looked up at her, staring daggers. 'You killed Ricky, didn't you?'

'He murdered Roxy, and you helped him.'

Devlin kicked him again in the stomach. He cried in pain, coughing up blood that had become trapped in his throat. Tears were welling in his eyes.

'Why did you kill her?' Devlin asked desperately.

'I just pointed the camera. It was Patrick's idea. If anyone deserves to die, it's him.'

Of course, Devlin thought. Jordan and Ricky couldn't do anything without his direction.

'Why her? Why did you choose her?' she screamed.

'I don't know. We didn't choose her. She was just another whore.'

'No,' Devlin said, shaking her head. 'She was my friend.'

She raised the hammer.

'No, please,' Jordan cried, raising a weak hand to try and protect himself.

The hand did nothing. The hammer crashed down onto his skull, and he collapsed to the floor. The spectacles pinged from his face and cracked against the wall. Devlin continued to beat at his head multiple times, blood splashing up at her face and onto the glass window.

She stopped to catch her breath staring at Jordan's motionless body lying in a pool of blood. Two down, but now there was a third. Patrick. He would need to pay as well. She was about to leave when she glimpsed through the glass window to see the young girl being groped by a large sweaty naked man in his forties. She looked in horror as the girl tried to get away, but he held her back, forcefully pinning her down on the bed.

Devlin left the booth and looked up the corridor to where the curtain was separating her from the gauntman. She looked the other way to find a door with a sign reading "PRIVATE". She headed through the door and came upon a switch box on the wall marked "CURTAIN CONTROLS". She switched it from "OPEN" to "CLOSE".

She made her way through another door and found herself inside the central room surrounded by the viewing windows now sealed off by the curtains. She approached the bed in the centre, the man with his back toward her leaning over the young girl like a predator ready to feast.

Devlin crept up behind him, and without hesitation, she brought the hammer down onto his back, cracking his spine. He screamed in agony, collapsing to the floor and trying to crawl away, clutching his back with one hand. Devlin swung the hammer into the side of his head, and he collapsed unconscious. The killing was so easy to her now; she was becoming numb to it.

Devlin pulled a blanket from the bed and wrapped it around the shivering young girl. She helped her to her feet and led her out of the room. Devlin opened the private door, but their path was blocked by the many men who had exited their booths to complain about the show ending too soon. The gaunt man appeared at the curtain to see what the problem was.

Devlin shut the door and looked down at the girl.

'Hey, is there another way out of here?'

The girl struggled to open her eyes to look around.

Devlin took a chance on one last door near them and entered. They climbed a long staircase, the girl's feet dragging up the steps. They reached a door at the top, and Devlin opened it cautiously. She was surprised to be met with an inflatable sex doll in front of her and almost jumped out of her skin.

They were in an adult sex shop. It was silent, a couple of men browsing the merchandise on offer. The shop assistant was behind the counter reading a magazine, oblivious to their appearance from the door.

Devlin guided the girl to the main door, and they slipped out quietly before anyone could notice them.

#

The gaunt man was irritated. He'd had to give refunds to everyone, and now one of the viewers hadn't left his booth. He banged loudly on the door.

'Come on, shows over, mate. Don't make me come in there and find you still tugging away. Otherwise, I'm going to cut your dick off,' he said.

There was no answer, so he knocked again. He knew they were never going to answer, so he risked the awkwardness and pushed open the door. He was a man who had witnessed many horrors, and so the sight of Jordan's broken skull and the blood didn't faze him, but it was a surprise.

'Fuck me,' he said. 'Paul, get over here.'

Paul rushed over to him, panting. He was a short stumpy man with a shaved head and wide eyes. He looked in the door at the mess.

'Oh shit, another one?' Paul said.

The gaunt man turned to Paul with confusion on his face.

'What do you mean another one?'

'Don's dead, and the girl's gone.'

'Shit,' the gaunt man replied.

'What do you think happened?' Paul asked.

'Fucked if I know. Dump the bodies far from here. The last thing we need is the police sniffing around.'

The gaunt man watched as Paul stepped into the room and attempted to lift Jordan's body.

Devlin took the young girl to the nearest hospital and left her outside the entrance. She didn't want to leave her alone, but Devlin was covered in blood, and there would no doubt be questions if the staff saw her. As Devlin was about to leave, the young girl grabbed her wrist.

'Thank you,' she struggled to say.

Devlin nodded and then disappeared into the night.

#

Devlin burst into her apartment, slamming the door shut behind her. She pulled the blonde wig from her head, tossed it to the side and stumbled over to the bedside drawer. It was like deja vu. She needed another fix, her nerves were shredded, and she didn't know how much longer she could hold out.

Devlin took the tin from the drawer and began her methodical preparation process. Once the needle was in her arm and injected its coolness, she calmed.

Her memories of Roxy were fading, but the drug helped make them clearer. To her, it was like travelling back in time and reliving the moments minute by minute. Everything was sharper and more powerful, the smells, sounds and feelings.

She wasn't sure she could kill those men when the thought of murder came to mind, but she was sure Roxy had faith in her. Roxy always encouraged her and gave her confidence. She remembered the day she convinced her to become an escort. Devlin wasn't sure she could do that either, but Roxy had this ability to make you believe you were capable of anything.

When Devlin stepped out of the bathroom wearing a pink cocktail dress and twirled in front of Roxy like a catwalk model, Roxy knew Devlin had it in her.

'Don't be silly,' Devlin said at the mere suggestion.

'You've got what it takes,' Roxy replied. 'Believe me, I didn't think I could do it, but then I found I had the knack. After a while, I started to enjoy it, plus the money doesn't hurt.'

There was just something missing, Roxy thought as she looked Devlin up and down with a thoughtful finger on her lips. She needed to make Devlin stand out from the competition. A trademark that clients will remember.

She rummaged through a drawer and took out a box of pink hair dye. Devlin wasn't sure she wanted pink hair. She was fond of her brunette locks, but Roxy reassured her it would just be a few streaks on one side. Once again, Roxy had convinced Devlin to take a plunge, and she was right. Devlin loved her hairstyle and ever since maintained the pink dye. Clients would comment on it, and she became renowned for it. She missed that guidance, that comforting hand that would push her forward but also catch her if she fell.

CHAPTER 18

The bedroom had an expensive classical style with iconic film posters on the walls, such as *Citizen Kane*, *La Dolce Vita* and *A Fistful of Dollars*. The black furniture popped off the white walls giving it a simplistic feel.

Patrick lay asleep in bed next to a woman with smeared make-up and tussled hair. She awoke, looked over at him, smiling with affection, and then quietly slipped out of the bed, pulling on a crumpled dress from the floor. She collected up a pair of high-heeled shoes and approached a desk where she scribbled a note on a pad and tore it out, placing it on the bedside table next to Patrick. She kissed him softly on the cheek and quietly left the bedroom.

The sound of the front door opening and closing was heard. Patrick snapped open his eyes. He had been awake for twenty minutes but didn't want to suffer the awkwardness of morning conversation with a one-night stand. He climbed out of bed wearing only his underwear and looked down at the note. He picked it up and read it. "I had a great night. Call me, love June," it read.

Patrick smirked. He scrunched up the note and tossed it in a nearby rubbish bin. He wasn't the type for relationships. He had a simple need, and when it was satisfied, he wasn't interested anymore.

He walked over to a mirrored wardrobe and slid open the door to reveal a large camcorder on a tripod hidden inside. He ejected the tape and, taking a pen, wrote the name "June" on the label.

He pulled open the top drawer of a dresser to reveal several other tapes lined up in unison. Each one had a woman's name written on the label. He may not wish to see them in person again, but a quick reminder of their performance was always welcome. Who knows, if he was ever desperate for a new performer, he had a catalogue of potential candidates to review. He added the new tape to the collection and then ran his fingers over the edge of each one until he came to a tape with a red "X" on the label. He carefully closed the drawer smiling to himself.

CHAPTER 19

The police canteen was silent. The breakfast rush had been and gone, and only Lewis remained sat at a table in the centre of the room. He had a full English in front of him, but he merely stared at it, pushing the sausage around the plate with his fork.

He was still hung up on the night he tried to kiss Devlin. Why did he do it? He knew how vulnerable she was, and he took advantage of that. He felt awful and wondered how he could make it up to her if she would ever let him. Solving this case would be a start. There was no doubt Ricky was the man who held the knife, but who were the other two involved? There were plenty of suspects at Hardwood Films, top of the list being Patrick, but until they had that search warrant, it was going to be difficult to break him.

Grantham sat down opposite him, placing a case file on the table to try and catch his attention. Lewis reluctantly looked up at him.

'What are you moping for?' Grantham asked.

Lewis put the fork down and pushed the plate away. He sat back in his chair.

'Nothing, it's personal,' he replied.

'Well, put your problems to one side for a minute and listen. We've got our search warrant for the film studio.'

'That came through quickly.'

'It was fast-tracked.'

'Why?'

'Another body was found in the early hours of this morning, identified as Jordan Waits. Otherwise known as the cameraman employed by Hardwood Films.'

Grantham now had Lewis's full attention noticing his posture straighten as he listened much more enthusiastically.

'There were markings on his arm,' Grantham said, flipping over the cover of the case file and removing a photograph. He passed it to Lewis, who studied the image of an arm tattooed with the pattern of letters and numbers.

'These are the markings seen in the tape. He filmed it?' Lewis said.

'This is too much of a coincidence. These two murders are connected, and they must be connected to the dead girl. I think someone is picking off those responsible.'

Lewis considered Grantham's theory with interest.

'I think it's your friend,' Grantham added.

'Devlin?'

Grantham nodded. 'She has a motive.'

Lewis shook his head in disbelief.

'She can't be the killer. She has no idea who these men are or the connection. It's not possible,' he protested.

Grantham rested his elbows on the table, clasping his hands together and locking his fingers. He leant in closer.

'CCTV footage from a nightclub Romero was at the night of his murder shows he left with a young girl,' he said.

'That could have been anyone.'

'Granted, but it *could* be her. Whomever this girl is, the detectives on the case want to speak to her. They don't know about Devlin yet, but I'm going to advise they bring her in for questioning.'

'Wait, this is crazy. You're not… you don't know her like I do. She's not capable of something like that,' Lewis said, the desperation in his voice all too obvious.

'Nobody is until they're pushed. And she was pushed pretty hard. Seeing the contents of that tape couldn't have helped.'

Lewis tried to think how to convince Grantham otherwise, but he knew it was futile. When Grantham had an idea in his head, it stuck like glue, and there was no persuading him otherwise.

'Let me speak to her first before they barge in throwing their weight around and scaring her. Please, give me that at least,' Lewis said.

Grantham pondered his request. He didn't like Lewis acting so audacious toward him, especially when he was letting his personal feelings get in the way of a murder case, but he also had a heart, and looking into Lewis's puppy dog eyes, he felt it melt.

'Normally, I wouldn't even consider a request like that, but as it's you, I'll keep quiet for now. But you talk to her as soon as possible. I don't want to be sitting on this for too long.'

Lewis thanked Grantham and stood up so quickly the chair toppled over behind him. He was about to rush past Grantham when the old man extended a hand and held him back. Lewis looked down at his superior's furrowed brows.

'Don't get too close, Lewis. It didn't end well last time.'

Lewis nodded, and happy the words had got through, Grantham removed his hand to allow his excitable partner to leave. After watching Lewis disappear through the door, the ageing detective pulled the plate of food over to him and tucked into the sausage with vigour.

CHAPTER 20

The cast and crew were ready and raring to go, but they were all waiting for Jordan, whom Devlin knew would never show. Stephanie and Chantelle sat in director's chairs reading glamour magazines. Not far from them was Mike rolling a joint on his knee spilling cannabis grains onto the polished floor.

Josie was sitting by Devlin, talking to her, but all Devlin could hear was noise. Her attention was hooked on Patrick pacing up and down with frustration at the absence of his cameraman.

'Okay,' Patrick said. 'I don't know where he is, but we're wasting time sitting around. I'm going to shoot the scene myself. Rose.'

Devlin felt Patrick's eyes lock onto her. Josie had stopped talking, much to her relief. She didn't want to seem rude; she liked Josie, but she needed to be focused, and her constant jabbering was becoming a nuisance.

Devlin stood and approached Patrick. She had been dressed in a skimpy top and hot pants, and her face was caked in make-up.

'Okay, you know the scene, right?' Patrick asked.

Devlin nodded.

'Don't be nervous. Just enjoy it,' he continued, placing his hands on Devlin's shoulders and rubbing them gently. Devlin glanced down at his hairy knuckles and tried to hide her grimace. She didn't want this man touching her, but she couldn't blow her cover. She needed to keep him right where she wanted him.

'Okay, everyone, let's shoot this.'

Patrick clapped his hands, and everyone got into their places. Devlin sat down on the bed and waited nervously.

Mike brushed away the debris from his trouser leg and cradled the joint on top of his ear for later. He picked up a set of headphones connected to a sound recorder, placed them on his head and positioned himself holding out a boom microphone.

Ricky's replacement, the famous John Biggs, made his way onto the set and stood behind a fake door, ready to enter the scene. He was a slimmer man than Ricky, clearly not a fan of the gym, but what he lacked in girth, he made up for in height at six foot five. A huge name in adult entertainment, Patrick had blown the rest of his budget to cast him, certain he would recoup the costs in sales.

Patrick approached a camcorder on a tripod and pressed the record button. He checked the viewfinder and adjusted it to focus on Devlin. Chantelle watched on, staring daggers at her.

'Okay, rolling. Action!' Patrick shouted.

John entered through the fake door. He made his way over to Devlin and sat down next to her. They exchanged some cheesy lines of dialogue Patrick had hastily written before John placed a hand on Devlin's leg rubbing it gently. He waited for her to reciprocate, but Devlin froze up. She looked around at the many pairs of eyes watching her and found her body failing her. She couldn't do it.

Patrick waited for her to interact and move the scene forward, but the longer it went on, the lower his brows went.

'Cut!' Patrick shouted. 'Rose, what's the problem? You need to do something. You can't just sit there. Okay, still rolling. Action!'

'Wait!' Devlin burst out.

Patrick stopped recording. 'What is it?'

'I can't do this,' Devlin whispered.

'Oh, for fuck's sake. Okay, everyone, take a break.'

Mike put down the boom mic and took a seat. John slinked off set with frustration and sparked up a conversation with Chantelle, who was excited by his presence.

Patrick took John's place sitting next to Devlin, his shoulder rubbing up against hers.

'What's the matter?' he said quietly.

'I just don't think I can go through with this,' she replied.

She thought she could do it, but the sight of all these people gawping at her was too much to bear. Maybe there was another way she could get to Patrick if he decided to fire her.

'Look, Rose. I know this is your first time, and you're nervous, but we need to shoot this scene today. I'm already behind schedule, and I can't afford to waste more time like this.'

Devlin stared off into the distance. Patrick could see he wasn't getting through to her and so he slung an arm around her shoulder and pulled her in close. He spoke quietly into her ear. She felt his warm breath on her neck, disgusted by it.

'If I don't finish this shoot today, I'm going to lose a lot of money that I've already invested. My distributors are waiting on this film, and they won't wait forever. Please don't force me to use more persuasive methods. You wouldn't be the first.'

Patrick squeezed Devlin's wrist tightly. She winced in pain, looking up at his scowling eyes.

'Do you understand?' he asked.

Devlin knew very well what he meant. She'd witnessed first-hand what he was capable of. He wasn't going to let her leave, not without shooting this scene first, and there was no way for her to escape. She couldn't rely on anyone here to help her if she tried. Who knows, maybe they were all involved in Roxy's death, and they would be just as comfortable forcing her to his demands. She'd foolishly put herself in this position, and now she would have to suffer the consequences just to save further punishment. She subtly nodded at Patrick, and he grinned with relief releasing his hand from her wrist.

Patrick stood up and clapped his hands to gain everyone's attention.

'Okay. Let's get back to it. Rose is ready. Pick it up from your entry, John.'

Everybody hastily returned to their positions.

Josie sidled up to Devlin and whispered in her ear. 'Just pretend he's someone else. Someone you like. It makes it a whole lot easier,' Josie said with a sweet smile before scurrying away.

Devlin smiled. Maybe she did have one friend here, at least. She'd still be outnumbered though if she tried anything and prepared herself for what might come.

'Rolling. Action!' Patrick shouted.

John re-entered and sat down next to Devlin. They exchanged their lines of dialogue, and John placed his firm hand on her leg. She then placed her hand on his rough stubbled cheek and leaned in to kiss him. She closed her eyes and thought of Roxy. She was doing this all for her, and it would be worth it in the end.

Patrick stared into the viewfinder and grinned, pleased at the footage he was getting.

#

Lewis knocked again, louder this time, but there was still no answer.

'Devlin, if you're in there, open the door,' he called out.

A deep voice behind him spoke, 'She's not in.'

Lewis turned to see a middle-aged caretaker in overalls halfway up a wooden step ladder. He was changing a light bulb.

'She went out this morning,' the caretaker said, screwing in the new bulb and bringing light to the hallway.

'Do you have a key for her front door?' Lewis asked.

'I do,' the caretaker said, climbing down the step ladder and wiping his hands on a cloth giving Lewis an incredulous look. 'Do you expect me to just let you in?'

Lewis took out his police ID and flashed his badge, the polished chrome glistening in the light of the caretaker's new bulb.

'Yeah, I do,' Lewis replied.

'Oh, fair enough,' the caretaker said, dropping his head in embarrassment. He made his way over to Devlin's apartment door and fumbled with a bunch of keys hooked on his belt. He selected the correct one and unlocked the door.

'There you go, Officer.'

'Thank you,' Lewis said, pushing the door open.

'Do you need anything else?'

'No, it's fine. Thank you again.'

Lewis closed the door behind him, and the caretaker returned to his errands, slightly put off by his rudeness.

Lewis knew he was crossing a line, searching someone's home without a warrant or any clear reason to suspect them, but Grantham's theory had got to him. He wanted to be sure Devlin wasn't capable of murdering two men, and if he didn't find any evidence to the contrary, he could at least relax in the knowledge he was right about her.

He began opening drawers and cupboards, hunting for potential murder weapons. The coroner claimed the same object killed both victims, so it was possible it was an item Devlin already had in her possession and still has.

He checked under the bed and then pulled open the bedside table. He found the pencil case inside and flipped open the lid finding her drug paraphernalia. He shook his head in disappointment. He suspected she was dealing with Roxy's death a lot easier than the average person, and now he knew why. She was numbing herself to the pain. He put the case down and continued his search.

#

'Cut!' Patrick shouted.

He stopped the camcorder recording and switched it off.

'That's a wrap. Good stuff,' he said with a delighted smile

John climbed out of the bed and picked up a dressing gown putting it on though he seemed more comfortable strutting around completely naked. Devlin still lay in the bed, the covers pulled up to her neck and a traumatised look on her face. Everyone was still staring at her. Josie approached with a dressing gown.

'Here you go,' she said.

Devlin slid out from under the covers, covering herself, and pulled on the gown, Josie helping her.

'You did good,' Josie said with a warm smile.

Devlin forced a smile back and made her way with haste to the dressing room, closing the door behind her. Josie looked on with concern.

Devlin tiptoed around the clothes scattered across the floor toward a dressing table complete with theatre-style mirrors. Make-up and other beauty products cluttered the surface. Devlin sat down and stared at her reflection, the lights around the edge of the mirror glowing on her distraught face. She attempted to replay everything in her head, but it was like an out-of-body experience, and she couldn't remember exactly what she had done. She could always rewatch it. Patrick now had her on tape, just like Roxy.

Devlin grabbed her nearby handbag and rushed over to the toilet door, but found her path blocked by Chantelle.

'Still trying to wash the blood from your hands?' Chantelle sneered.

'Get out of my way,' Devlin said, trying to go around her.

Chantelle grabbed Devlin's shoulders and pushed her up against the wall.

'Where's Jordan?' she said, shoving her face into Devlin's to raise the intimidation. 'Did you kill him as well?'

'Leave me alone.' Devlin attempted to break free from Chantelle's grip but felt her apply more pressure, pinning her to the wall.

'Don't you think it's a bit of a coincidence that as soon as you start working here, one person winds up dead and another goes missing?' Chantelle said.

'I don't know what you're talking about.'

'No? Maybe there's some evidence in your handbag that could prove otherwise.'

Chantelle tried to snatch Devlin's handbag from her, but she clutched on tight. As they struggled, the handbag slipped from both their grips and tumbled onto the floor, almost spilling its contents.

Devlin lost her temper, and she could feel the fury building inside. Before she knew it, her hand was around Chantelle's throat, throwing her up against the wall. A look of shock came over the actress's face as she stared into Devlin's threatening eyes. She grasped at her throat, feeling her air supply restricted.

'If you really think I'm a murderer, do you think it wise to piss me off? You wouldn't want to be my next victim, would you?' Devlin hissed through gritted teeth.

Tears welled in Chantelle's eyes as she tried to pull Devlin's hand from her neck.

'Is everything okay?' Josie's voice said behind Devlin.

Devlin released Chantelle, and she dropped to the floor, gasping for air. Devlin picked up her handbag and entered the toilet slamming the door shut behind her.

'What's going on?' Josie asked Chantelle.

The wounded girl didn't reply. She pulled herself to her feet and pushed past Josie exiting the room.

#

Devlin sat down on the toilet and took a deep breath. She didn't know whom she was becoming. Had she really just threatened Chantelle? She could risk everything and never have a chance of killing Patrick. She needed to make sure she didn't lose herself and stay in control. Luckily she had the perfect antidote.

She took out a syringe from her handbag, placing it gently on the edge of the sink. Rolling up the sleeve of the dressing gown, she wrapped a belt taken from her handbag around her arm and yanked it tight. She pulled off the needle cover and injected herself. Releasing the belt, she sat back against the cistern behind her and felt calm again.

The first time she'd experienced violence, Devlin was on the receiving end of it. She had not long started escorting under Roxy's tutelage when she returned home battered and bruised. Her lip was cut, her nose bleeding, her dress torn, and her hair tussled. As soon as Roxy saw her in such a state, she rushed over from the bed where she was nestled reading a magazine.

Roxy guided Devlin over to the bed and sat her down. She then heard the story of what had happened.

He seemed like any other client, soft-spoken and a little shy, but when they arrived at the hotel, he began acting aggressively toward Devlin. She warned him rough play was not on the menu, but he didn't listen. Before she knew it, he was on top of her, and she couldn't move. Then the slaps started, before punching and kicking. All she could think was, *I want Roxy. Where's Roxy?*

Roxy listened with great difficulty, her mind conjuring images she didn't want to see. If she'd known his true self, she never would have sent Devlin to him.

Devlin burst into tears, her body still shaking with nerves. Roxy wrapped both arms around her and pulled her in close. She promised she would never let anything happen to her again and hoped Devlin could forgive her.

They looked into each other's eyes, feeling a calm fall over them. Devlin leant forward, kissing Roxy softly on the lips. Roxy pulled back, startled by this display of passion, but she couldn't deny she felt the same. She kissed Devlin back, and they fell onto the bed in a warm embrace. That was the day they fell in love.

CHAPTER 21

Patrick liked to have the television on in the background while he worked in his office. The consistent noise helped him focus while he sorted through the paperwork. However, this time it became a distraction when he glanced up to see a photograph of Jordan on the screen.

He snatched up the remote and increased the volume, the voice of a news reporter filling the room.

'The body of Jordan Waits was discovered at around 7 a.m. this morning by a local resident. Beaten to death by a blunt object, it is believed he was murdered at another location and his body dumped in this alleyway,' the reporter said as he gestured toward the alleyway he was standing in. 'Police suspect the murder is connected to that of adult film actor Ricky Romero. Both Romero and Waits were employed at Hardwood Films in West London.'

Footage of outside the film studio appeared on screen, and Patrick made his way closer to the television in astonishment.

'CCTV footage of Romero leaving a nightclub the night of his death with a young woman has been released by police. They are asking anyone who has information regarding her identity to come forward,' the reporter continued as black and white grainy footage at about one frame per second showed Ricky and Devlin stepping out the main door of the nightclub.

Patrick was now inches from the screen, trying to get a clearer look at the woman with Ricky. There was something familiar about her. Then it hit him. He looked through the windows of his office at Devlin, who had just exited the dressing room, now dressed and ready to leave. He turned back to the screen one last time and could see the resemblance.

But why? *Of course*, he thought. That's where he'd seen her before. She was there that night, standing outside the bar when he picked up Roxy. Different hair colour, but the face was no doubt the same. Everything was starting to fit now. That's why she wanted a job here, to get close to Ricky and Jordan, but what about him? Did she know he was involved? She was still here, so she must suspect others were. He needed to end her before she had a chance to get to him. He wouldn't go down without a fight.

He rushed out of his office and called out. 'Rose!'

Devlin stopped and turned to him, putting on one of the smiles she had become so good at faking. Patrick approached with hands together as if praying.

'I just wanted to apologise if I came across as pushy earlier today, but as you can probably understand, business is pressure,' he said. 'And I don't handle pressure well. You did a great job today. I think the scene is going to turn out perfect. I see a bright future for you in this industry.' He paused. 'Listen, I was wondering if maybe you'd like to come by mine tonight for dinner. As an apology and a little celebration of your performance.'

Devlin couldn't help but grin now. This was the chance she was hoping for, and he was giving it to her for free.

'I'd love to,' she replied.

'Excellent,' Patrick said, taking out a business card from his wallet and a pen from his pocket. He scribbled an address down on the card and passed it to her.

'Come by eight o'clock?'

'I'll be there,' she said, placing the business card in her handbag. She turned with a flick of her hair and walked away.

Devlin was about to reach the main entrance door when they burst open, and uniformed police officers entered with intent in their stride. Grantham followed close behind, enjoying the power he had. Devlin's heart was in her mouth. Was this it? Had they found out what she'd done? She ducked to one side, avoiding the impending authority as they headed into the centre of the room.

Patrick approached Grantham, confused by their presence.

'What the hell is going on?' he asked, aggravated.

'We have our search warrant, Mr Levesque,' Grantham replied, holding up a document. Patrick snatched it from him and read it.

'Do you have to do this now? We're in the middle of shooting.'

'I don't know if you're aware, Mr Levesque, but another employee of yours was found dead this morning.'

'I just saw it on the news. Is that what this is about?'

'Unfortunately, no. His death is no concern of mine, much like your late star. Although it has come to light that he, like Mr Romero, was possibly involved in the death of Roxanne Campbell. As you can imagine, employees of yourself being involved in a murder make this place very suspicious, and we suspect there was a third individual. Therefore we'd like to do a thorough search of these premises and interview all of your employees. We'd also like a DNA sample from everyone to eliminate them from our enquiries.'

'This is ridiculous,' Patrick exhaled.

Grantham turned to his waiting officers.

'Get searching. Look everywhere. Leave no stone unturned.'

They spread out like insects making their way into the dressing room and editing room. Grantham turned back to Patrick with a grin on his face. 'Do you mind if we use your office to conduct interviews?' he asked, enjoying himself a little too much.

Patrick was about to speak before Grantham cut him off.

'Excellent. I want all employees to gather in the centre of the room. Nobody leaves. I think we'll start with you, Mr Levesque.'

A couple of officers herded the cast and crew toward the bed. Devlin had managed to slip into a corner of darkness, and so far, nobody had spotted her. An officer passed by, but she was quick to duck down and avoid being seen.

She watched as Grantham led Patrick into his office and closed the door behind him. She needed to escape. She couldn't risk being seen. It wouldn't take long for them to figure out who she was, and the pieces would start coming together. She would miss her chance to kill Patrick.

She quietly crept through the studio using crates and equipment as cover, making her way toward the rear door of the building, but with officers moving around, it was going to be slow and difficult.

Meanwhile, Grantham had made himself comfortable behind Patrick's desk with a notepad laid out on the desk in front of him. Patrick sat awkwardly in a chair opposite. He didn't like that his office had been commandeered like this. It was his sanctum, and it was being tainted.

'Were you aware of Jordan Waits' past?' Grantham asked.

'As a matter of fact, I was,' Patrick replied.

'Two accusations of sexual abuse. Was it wise to employ him here?'

'They were just accusations, Detective. He was never convicted. He was a good cameraman. That's all that mattered to me.'

'But not the safety of the many women who work here?'

'I didn't mean that. You're twisting my words.'

'Then what did you mean?'

'Look, Jordan had issues mentally. He wasn't quite all there. He may have creeped out one or two people, but we never had an incident involving him or any of the girls. As far as I was concerned, he was harmless.'

'Until now. I think we can safely say Jordan's true nature has been exposed. And quite frankly, that raises many questions about yourself as you've so vehemently defended him.'

'You still suspect I had some kind of involvement in this girl's death?' Patrick said incredulously.

'It's my job to suspect everyone.'

'I've got nothing to hide, and your men aren't going to find any incriminating evidence to the contrary. You're wasting your time.'

Grantham stared at Patrick, disappointed. He knew it would be difficult to break Patrick if he was guilty, but he was giving nothing away. Perhaps he wasn't involved after all. Then again, talking to some of his employees may reaffirm those suspicions.

#

Devlin was pinned down behind a crate of camera equipment, a police officer searching a unit of drawers between her and the rear exit. He finished his hunt, finding nothing of interest, and walked away. Devlin took her chance rushing for the door, but before she could get there, Chantelle had stepped in her way.

'And where do you think you're going?' Chantelle said, venom in her voice.

Devlin refused to answer her question and tried to push past her, but Chantelle was steadfast.

'We were told not to leave. Do you have something to hide?' Her voice was so loud Devlin was worried someone would hear.

'Please, Chantelle. Just let me go. You don't understand,' Devlin pleaded.

'I'm not letting you go anywhere. In fact, I think we should go talk to that detective.'

Chantelle grabbed Devlin's hand and attempted to pull her, but Devlin snatched her hand back, and it slipped from Chantelle's grip.

'Just back off,' Devlin said, pushing Chantelle and causing her to trip over a cable behind her and fall flat on her rear. An arm swung out to catch herself, and on the way, camera lenses were knocked from a nearby shelf and clattered to the floor with a loud noise.

A police officer appeared from around the corner to see what the commotion was and caught Devlin standing over a dazed Chantelle.

'What's going on over here?' the officer called out.

Devlin did not hesitate to run for the back exit, the officer chasing after her.

Devlin pushed through the fire door and out onto an alleyway. A couple of officers were standing by a squad car, sneaking a cigarette break. Their attention was drawn by the slam of the door against the adjacent wall, encouraging them to stub out their cigarettes and chase after Devlin when she sprinted past them.

She exited the alleyway onto the main high street, the two officers hot on her heels following her into a crowded marketplace. Devlin slipped in between the bustling shoppers until she'd blended in, and the officers were at a loss as to where she'd gone. Before they had a chance to locate her, she had already broken free from the herd of people and ducked down a narrow alleyway. The two officers soon gave up and returned to the studio.

#

Grantham and Patrick approached the crowd gathered around Chantelle, who was lifted to her feet by an officer.

'What's going on?' Grantham asked.

'One of the girls left, sir,' a uniformed officer replied.

'Who?'

'Rose Charm,' Chantelle said, rubbing the back of her head. 'She killed Ricky. That's why she ran.'

'What makes you think that?' Grantham asked curiously.

'She was with him the night he died.'

'What does this girl look like?'

'Patrick has a photo of her in his office,' Chantelle said, gesturing toward Patrick.

'I'm going to need to see that photo,' Grantham said to Patrick.

Patrick reluctantly nodded. He was hoping to deal with this girl himself, but now it seemed the police would get to her first.

Grantham followed Patrick back to the office and watched as he took a polaroid off a pinboard and passed it to him. Grantham studied the photograph with interest. It was Devlin all right, just as he had suspected.

CHAPTER 22

Devlin was out of breath as she pushed open the front door of her apartment and slammed it shut behind her. She didn't have a chance to calm herself, though, as Lewis was sitting at the dining table staring at her.

'What are you doing here?' she asked. Her eyes shifted down to the pencil case in front of him.

She rushed over and snatched it toward her. 'Why are you going through my stuff?'

'That's not good for you,' he replied, gesturing toward the case with a nod of his head.

'Is that why you're here? To check up on me? Or were you hoping to finish what you started last time?'

Lewis wanted to react, but he stayed calm. He continued to stare at her, his brows low and intimidating.

'Do you know someone by the name of Jordan Waits?' he asked.

Devlin shook her head. She made her way over to the bedside table and returned the pencil case to its drawer. She sat down on the edge of the bed and looked down at the charm bracelet.

'He was found dead this morning,' Lewis continued. 'He worked at the same film studio as Ricky Romero.'

'So?'

'So, the two murders are connected, and they were both involved in Roxy's death.'

'Oh,' Devlin said, trying to feign surprise.

'Don't play dumb, Devlin,' Lewis shook his head. 'Just tell me, did you kill them?'

Devlin reluctantly looked at him.

'No. I couldn't do something like that.'

'Romero was seen leaving a nightclub with a young woman the night of his death. She looked an awful lot like you. So, I'll ask you again, did you kill them?'

Devlin shook her head, hoping it would be enough to appease him. She wanted this line of questioning to stop and for Lewis to leave. She had to meet Patrick tonight and needed to prepare.

'Then how do you explain this?' Lewis lifted his hand from under the table to reveal a blood-stained hammer, held in his grip between a piece of tissue. He placed it down on the table surface. Devlin hung her head and closed her eyes. It was all over. She had been found out.

'What were you thinking, Devlin? This is no way to get justice,' Lewis said.

'I was thinking they killed my friend,' she snapped back.

'You should have come to me as soon as you found out.'

'Why? So you could arrest them, send them to prison and then they'll be free again one day? No. Roxy doesn't have the luxury of getting her life back, so why should they? You saw what they did to her.'

'How did you find them?'

'I recognised Ricky in another film by the studio. So, I got a job there.'

'What kind of job?'

'What do you think?'

Lewis shook his head in disbelief. 'Jesus, Devlin.' And then something dawned on him. 'I thought I saw you there that day. I thought my mind was playing tricks on me.'

'I'm sorry I didn't tell you, okay? But I *had* to do it. For Roxy.'

'Well, now you *have* to turn yourself in.'

'No, I can't. Not until I've killed Patrick.'

'Patrick Levesque?'

Devlin nodded.

'He was involved? Do you have proof?' Lewis asked.

'Not yet. But Jordan told me it was Patrick's idea to kill Roxy. I don't know why, but I'm going to find out,' she replied with determination.

Lewis stood up, kicking the chair back behind him.

'No, you're not. We'll deal with him. And if you're not going to turn yourself in, I have to arrest you.'

Devlin jumped up from the bed and hastily walked over to him.

'Whose side are you on?'

'I'm on your side.'

'Then prove it.'

Devlin moved in close, placing her hands on Lewis's chest. She leaned in and kissed him. He reciprocated, but upon realizing what he was doing, pushed her away.

'No, Devlin. You're not going to get out of this. What you've done is wrong. I can't let that go!' he shouted.

Lewis reached into his coat pocket and dug out a pair of handcuffs. Devlin's head dropped. She had failed. But something inside her wouldn't give up. There had to be a way out of this. She glanced over at the bathroom.

'Can I at least take a shower first?' she asked.

'It's going to take a lot more than a shower to clean the blood from your hands.'

Devlin scowled at him.

'Go ahead,' he said. 'I'll be out here waiting. Don't take too long.'

Devlin entered the bathroom, closing the door behind her. Lewis heard the lock click into place. He sat down at the dining table, staring at the hammer. He rubbed his forehead in frustration, taking a deep breath.

#

It had been half an hour, and Lewis could still hear the sound of the shower running. He glanced at his watch and became suspicious. He approached the door pushing his ear up against it for any sign of life, but upon hearing none, he gently knocked.

'Devlin? You've been in there a while now. Hurry up.'

There was no reply. He knocked again, louder this time.

'Devlin? Devlin? Don't make me come in there.'

Still no response. Lewis grabbed the door handle, pushed it down, and rammed his shoulder against the door. After a few more tries, the bolt split through the wood of the frame, and the door swung open.

Lewis waved away the steam that had filled the room, trying to find Devlin amongst the fog. As the mist disappeared, he saw the window at the end of the room wide open.

'Shit.'

Lewis was about to turn and run, but he felt a heavy object hit him on the back of the head and everything went dark.

Devlin watched Lewis's body go limp and collapse to the tiled floor. She dropped the bathroom scales and looked down sorrowful at Lewis.

'I'm sorry,' she said.

She rummaged through his coat pocket and took out the handcuffs. She placed one cuff around his wrist and the other around a nearby radiator pipe. She turned off the shower and exited the bathroom. She collected the hammer from the table, placed it in her handbag, and headed for the door.

CHAPTER 23

Patrick was excited about the new 35-inch Mitsubishi television he'd obtained. He'd heard good things about the picture and sound quality, and now he'd managed to get a hold of one before it had even hit shelves in the UK. His contact in Japan had shipped it over to him for a discounted price to go along with a new VCR he had purchased.

Patrick untangled the many cables and began plugging them into the back of the VCR connecting it to the back of the television. To him, this was like surgery, ensuring every cable was neatly tucked away as he placed the device on the empty shelf of an entertainment unit.

He was keen to test out the new toy and began scanning a large wall of VHS tapes lined up neatly from floor to ceiling. It needed to be the right film that could test its limits.

It hadn't been the most enjoyable day with the police overturning the studio, but they hadn't found anything incriminating, at least. He'd been very careful about that. Now he could enjoy his evening with some finely crafted entertainment from Hollywood.

Before he had a chance to select an option, a knock at the door distracted him. He answered it surprised to find Devlin leant up against the door frame seductively.

'Hello,' Patrick said with a grin. 'Come in.'

He gestured with a wave of his hand, and Devlin stepped inside.

'I must say, I'm surprised to see you. I thought after today's incident you wouldn't come. You made a hasty exit when the police specifically asked you not to leave. You're a bad girl.'

'I'm not a fan of the police,' she replied as she made her way around the living room, studying his many film posters.

'Had a few run-ins with them in the past, have you?'

'Something like that.' She smirked.

'I like a girl with a dark side. We should explore that in one of my films sometime. Would you care for a glass of wine?'

'Please.'

'Take a seat,' Patrick said as he made his way into the kitchen.

Devlin sat down on the sofa and almost disappeared as she sank into it. Patrick returned quickly with two glasses of wine, passing one to her. As soon as she received it, she took a large gulp. Her mouth was becoming dry as the nerves built up inside her. He sat down next to her, throwing an arm casually over the back of the sofa.

'I'm so glad you decided to come. I was very impressed by your performance today,' he said, putting on the charm.

'So you said.'

'I see great things for you in the future. I thought maybe we could discuss some ideas this evening. I'm dying to hear your thoughts.'

'And I'd kill to hear yours.'

Patrick held up his glass. 'To exciting futures.'

Devlin clinked her glass against his in a toast, and both of them took a sip, neither willing to take their eyes off the other.

'I was just about to review one of my latest films,' he said, placing the glass down. 'Would you care to take a look? I'd like to get your opinion.'

'Sure.'

Devlin took another gulp of the wine before placing the glass down on the coffee table. Patrick disappeared into the bedroom momentarily before returning with a VHS tape in his hand.

'I think you'll like it. It's something I'm very proud of,' he said, placing the tape in his new VCR and pressing play.

Devlin watched the screen with interest. Her heart rate increased when it became clear the film he was showing her. Roxy was sitting on the bed moments before her death. Devlin looked over at Patrick to find he was staring at her with devilish eyes.

'She was one of the best actresses I've ever seen. Her performance was so real.'

'You bastard,' Devlin cried.

She reached into her handbag, took out the hammer, and stood up, ready to attack him, but she barely made it halfway before she started feeling light-headed and paused.

'Are you okay?' Patrick said, feigning concern.

Devlin tried to focus on him, but the room was swaying from side to side, and her eyelids were becoming heavy.

'Here, let me take that from you,' Patrick said as he pulled the hammer from Devlin's limp hand and placed it down on the coffee table out of her reach.

She wanted to wrap her hands around his throat, but she no longer had control over her body. She felt weak, and her knees were trembling.

Devlin dropped, but Patrick reacted quickly, catching her in his arms, the blonde wig falling from her head.

'That's it. Just relax,' he said, lifting her. 'It will all be over soon.'

As she became unconscious, Devlin thought back to that day she came home battered and bruised. She just wanted to forget it ever happened, but Roxy refused to let it go. She eventually tracked the man down, baseball bat in hand. When she returned later, Devlin was surprised to see blood on the bat and specks on Roxy's face.

'I thought you were just going to scare him,' Devlin said.

Roxy tossed the bat to one side and grabbed Devlin's shoulders, staring deep into her eyes.

'Scaring will never be enough. If anyone hurts you, I'll hurt them. I expect you to do the same for me.'

Devlin had promised she would, but now she'd failed.

She could feel the cold leather beneath her cheek as she dipped in and out of consciousness. She assumed she was in the backseat of a car, Patrick's car. The soft murmur of the road flying underneath lulled her back to sleep.

When the car eventually stopped, Patrick lifted Devlin out and carried her over to the main doors of the film studio. As he stepped through, Devlin's arm swung, and the charm bracelet slipped off her wrist falling to the floor unnoticed.

CHAPTER 24

Lewis was dazed and confused as to why he was lying on the bathroom floor. His clothes had become damp from the steam that had now dissipated. He sat up and felt a pain in his head. He stroked the back of his scalp; it was wet with blood. He tried to move, but his shoulder yanked him back. He looked down at his cuffed wrist and remembered Devlin.

He called out to her, but there was no reply. She must have gone after Patrick. He needed to stop her before it was too late. He pulled at the cuffs, but the radiator pipe was secure. He managed to get to his feet and grabbed the radiator at both sides. He jerked it up and down, feeling the screws behind loosen from the wall.

One final tug and the screws slipped from their holes, and the radiator came free. He pulled and twisted until the pipe was bent and weakened. Eventually, it snapped, and he was able to slip the cuff from it and rush out of the room.

After a quick phone call to dispatch for the address, Lewis arrived at Patrick's apartment out of breath and concussed, hoping he was not too late. Using the blue lights of the unmarked Ford Sierra helped him avoid the late-night traffic, and he'd managed to get there within twenty minutes. He sprinted down the hallway to Patrick's front door and banged loudly with his fist.

'Mr Levesque. Please, open up. Mr Levesque!' Lewis shouted.

He waited impatiently, but there was no answer. He began thinking Devlin had already started the execution, which would explain the lack of reply, or worse, Patrick had overpowered her, and she was in danger.

Lewis took a step back. He lifted his right leg and lunged forward, thumping the sole of his foot into the door by the lock. The frame splintered, and the door swung open. He rushed inside and looked around, checking bedrooms and the bathroom, but there was no one home. As he was about to leave, he stepped on the television remote that was lying carelessly on the floor. The VCR started playing, and the image of Roxy's murder appeared on the screen. Lewis watched in horror. Devlin was right.

He exited the apartment to find a neighbour standing at their door, being nosey.

'What's with all the noise?' the neighbour cried angrily.

Lewis took out his badge showing it to them.

'I'm looking for Mr Levesque. Any idea where I might find him?' Lewis asked.

'Well, if he isn't home, he's probably working late. He does that a lot, coming home at God knows how early in the morning and waking me up '

Of course, Lewis thought. *The film studio. That's where he'll be.* He turned and bolted down the hallway back toward the elevator.

CHAPTER 25

The studio lights blinded her as she opened her eyes and tried to get her bearings. She felt something cutting into the corners of her mouth and realised she was gagged with a handkerchief and unable to scream. She tried to reach up with her hand, but her wrists were tied down with chafing rope.

Devlin glanced to her side, and as her eyes adjusted to the brightness, she saw Patrick sitting on a stool beside her, studying her hammer in his hands, picking at the dried flecks of blood on the head.

She pulled harder at her binds, but they were taut, just like the ones wrapped around her ankles, pinning her to the bed.

'You think you're so clever, but I know who you are now. I recognised you from the night I picked up your friend. I'll give you credit; up until this point, you've been very resourceful, infiltrating my studio to exact your revenge,' Patrick said with a sinister tone.

He stood and threw the hammer across the room. It bounced off the floor a couple of times before settling. He stuck his face into Devlin's and looked deep into her frightened eyes.

'I'm sure you're wondering why we killed your friend,' he said, his breath stinking of wine. 'The main reason is money. You don't understand how cutthroat this industry can be. Year after year, more competition and lower sales figures. I was almost at the end. I even looked into bankruptcy, but then I got a phone call. He wanted to see real death on camera and was willing to pay a significant sum for it. Enough to save this place.

And when you're that desperate, you'll do whatever it takes, no matter how dark and twisted. So I was willing to do it.'

Patrick looked off into the distance as if recalling a past train of thought.

'But when it came to choosing who? I thought of my brother who'd been paralysed by a fucking whore who beat the shit out of him with a baseball bat.' Patrick's eyes had now shifted back in Devlin's direction, piercing her with their scowl. 'It was like killing two birds with one stone. Well, killing one bird at least.'

Patrick began circling the bed around Devlin's feet, running his fingers softly against her bare toes. She attempted to free herself again, but it was futile. She was going nowhere.

'And now you've killed people important to me, and I can't let you get away with that. But, I won't let a good opportunity go to waste.'

Patrick approached a camcorder set up on a tripod, the lens pointing directly at Devlin. He adjusted the shot slightly. 'You're going to be the star of my next film. Sequels always make twice as much money,' he said with a grin, then moved back over to the stool by Devlin.

'Unfortunately, you won't be able to see the final edit,' Patrick continued, picking up a syringe from the bedside table and admiring it. 'Due to an unforeseen overdose.'

He placed the syringe carefully back down on the bedside table. Devlin then watched from the corner of her eye as he picked up a small plastic bag of white powder and waved it in front of her.

'By the way, thank you for providing me with the appropriate means. I'm sure when they find your body, the police will see no need to question any further.'

He dropped the bag back onto the table and pulled a white mask from the back pocket of his jeans. The very same one used by Ricky in Roxy's snuff film.

'But first things first. We wouldn't want to be identified now, would we?'

Patrick pulled the mask over his face, his eyes peering through the small holes keeping a tight focus on Devlin. He pressed record on the camcorder and started to climb onto the bed by her feet like a tiger hunting. Devlin desperately wanted to kick him, but her feet could only shuffle about.

A loud banging at the main doors forced Patrick to pause and look over his shoulder. The banging continued. He whipped off the mask, his hair tussled.

'Don't go anywhere,' he said.

He climbed off the bed, stuffing the mask back into his pocket, and collected a cable flex from a nearby trolley. Devlin wrestled around the bed. She had to use this chance before he got back.

Patrick unlocked the door and pulled it slightly ajar to see Lewis's soaking face poke in, torrential rain pouring behind him. Patrick hid the cable flex behind his back.

'Mr Levesque, can I come in?' Lewis shouted through the noise of the rain.

'I'm busy,' Patrick replied.

'Please, I'll only be a minute. Unless you have something to hide?'

Patrick gave a friendly smile and pulled the door wide open, allowing Lewis to step in from out of the wet weather.

'Well?' Patrick asked impatiently.

'I have reason to believe your life is in danger tonight. I think it best you come with me to the station until the suspect is in custody.'

'And why would my life be in danger?'

'I can explain on the way.'

Patrick looked into Lewis's eyes and suspected an ulterior motive.

'Thank you for your concern, Detective. I can take care of myself. I don't require your assistance,' Patrick said.

'I understand that, but for peace of mind.'

'No, I'm fine. Now, if you wouldn't mind leaving, I have things to do.' Patrick placed a hand on Lewis's shoulder and attempted to nudge him back out the door.

'But Mr Levesque—'

'If you do not leave, I will be forced to call your superior and report you for police harassment. I do not need your help, Detective. Goodbye.'

'Fine, but if at any point you feel your life is in danger, do not hesitate to call,' Lewis replied, offering his business card.

'I know the number to call. Goodbye, Detective.'

Lewis was tempted to arrest Patrick there and then, but without evidence, it wouldn't hold. Right now, the tape he found in Patrick's apartment was only circumstantial, and he found it after entering without a warrant. He needed something concrete to show he was involved. Instead, he would have to wait for Devlin to appear. He suspected she eventually would, and he could intercept her before she made things worse for herself. Then he and Grantham could deal with Patrick following the letter of the law.

Lewis turned to leave, but something glistening on the floor caught his eye. He bent down to pick up the charm bracelet and studied it with recognition. He was about to turn and say something when a cable flex began choking him. Patrick pulled his fists close together, tightening the flex around Lewis's neck. Lewis clutched at the makeshift garotte and managed to pull it forward enough to allow him to draw in a breath.

He used the small amount of energy he had left to throw an elbow backwards, catching Patrick in the gut and winding him. Patrick released his grip on the flex, allowing Lewis to pull it from his throat. He spun around, swinging a fist, and punched Patrick in the face, knocking him to the ground.

Lewis left him stunned and made his way through the second set of doors into the main studio space.

'Devlin?' he called out.

He spotted her tied to the bed and ran over to help. He pulled the gag from her mouth and was able to untie one hand when she called out:

'Lewis!'

Lewis saw Devlin's eyes looking past him and turned to see the blade of a box cutter coming toward his face. As Patrick swung the weapon, Lewis managed to dodge each swipe. He was forced to back up until he was trapped against one of the set's false walls.

Patrick went in for another lunge. Lewis ducked to the side, and the knife penetrated the plasterboard wall. Lewis took his chance and grabbed Patrick's arm, raising it high above them both. Lewis bashed the arm against the wall several times, Patrick cracking his knuckles. His fingers eventually opened, and the knife dropped to the floor.

The two men continued to wrestle with each other as Devlin untied herself from the bed. Patrick head-butted Lewis, breaking his nose, blood gushing down his chin. As he tried to compose himself, he felt Patrick's hands wrap around his throat and squeeze, thumbs pressing deep into his windpipe. He struggled for breath as he attempted to pull Patrick's hands free.

Before Lewis succumbed, Devlin appeared behind Patrick and stabbed him in the neck with the syringe pumping its contents into him.

Patrick released Lewis, letting him drop to his knees, gasping for air. He spun around, smacking Devlin across the face and knocking her to the ground. He pulled the syringe from his neck, tossing it aside.

Patrick approached the hammer on the floor and picked it up. He towered over a stunned Devlin, his shadow casting her in darkness.

'I think I'll give you the same courtesy you gave Ricky and Jordan,' Patrick said as he raised the hammer.

Devlin closed her eyes, waiting for the fatal blow, but all she heard was the sound of choking and the thud of the hammer hitting the floor. She opened her eyes and saw Patrick clutching at his throat, trying desperately to breathe. His eyes were wide open in a state of shock. His legs buckled, and he collapsed to the floor. She watched as he shook in some kind of seizure, foaming at the mouth. Then suddenly, he was still.

Devlin looked over at Lewis, who had just witnessed Patrick's death alongside her. She rushed over to him, wrapping her arms around his neck and pulling him close to her.

'I'm sorry. I didn't mean for you to get involved,' she said on the verge of tears.

'It's okay. I'm fine. Just go. I'll deal with this.'

Devlin looked at him with grateful eyes.

'Are you sure?' she asked.

'Go,' he simply replied.

Devlin stood and was about to leave via the main doors, but she paused. A thought came over her, something she needed to destroy. She ran over to the editing room and disappeared inside.

'Devlin, where are you going?' Lewis shouted.

Lewis appeared at the door, still nursing his bleeding nose, to find Devlin sorting through a drawer full of VHS tapes. She scanned the titles written on each label until she came to one that read "Scene 3: Rose & John". She took it out.

'What is that?' Lewis asked.

'Something I need to destroy.'

'Devlin, if that's evidence—'

'It's not,' she replied. 'You don't need to see it.'

Lewis looked into her sad eyes. He gave her an understanding nod and stepped aside. Devlin brushed past him out the door. He listened for the main doors to open and close and then wondered how he was going to explain this mess.

CHAPTER 26

Grantham soon arrived to find his partner sitting on the bed holding a bloody handkerchief to his nose. Uniformed officers appeared behind and secured the area. Lewis was admiring the charm bracelet in his hand as his superior approached, staring down at the corpse beside him.

'What happened?' Grantham asked, disappointment in his voice.

Lewis pocketed the bracelet and pulled the blood-stained cloth away from his nostrils to see if the bleeding had stopped.

'He was murdered,' Lewis replied nasally.

'I can see that. What were you doing here?'

'I had a suspicion his life may be in danger.' Lewis felt the blood begin to flow down his top lip again and plugged it with the handkerchief.

'And what may I ask aroused such a suspicion?'

'He was the third man involved in the murder of Roxanne Campbell.'

'Evidence?'

'I was informed.'

'By who?'

'An anonymous source.'

'Anonymous, of course.' Grantham nodded. 'So you came straight here?'

Lewis was finding it difficult to look at Grantham. The man was a bloodhound and could detect a lie instantly.

'I went to his home first, but he wasn't there. A neighbour suggested I come here. I found the door ajar. When I entered, I was knocked unconscious by someone. When I awoke, I found his body.'

'What a coincidence,' Grantham said. 'You come by to check on him right after he gets murdered. I knew you were something of a prodigy in the force, but I didn't realise you were clairvoyant as well.'

Lewis knew he needed to look Grantham in the eye if he was going to have any chance of being believed. He gave him a stern look.

'It's the truth,' he said as convincingly as possible.

Grantham looked around at the increasing number of officers walking about the crime scene organising the gathering of forensic evidence.

'Let's have a chat in private,' Grantham said, gesturing toward the editing room.

Grantham closed the door behind them, and Lewis knew he was going to get a lecture. He'd been in this situation a few times before, and it always ended with him giving Grantham what he wanted and promising he would not do it again. He had to stay strong, for Devlin.

'So, do you want to tell me the truth, or do you want to stick to your bullshit story?' Grantham asked, not willing to beat around the bush.

'I told you the truth.'

'It was Devlin, wasn't it?'

'I don't know. I didn't see them. I was knocked—'

'Knocked unconscious, so you said,' Grantham needed to try a different tactic. 'Did you know she'd been working here?'

Lewis glanced up at Grantham briefly.

'Oh,' he said.

'Oh? I must say, I was expecting more surprise in your reaction. Am I to assume you already knew that?'

Lewis needed to get out of this room. The longer this went on the more chance there was of him breaking. He glared at Grantham.

'I don't know what you want from me.'

Grantham exhaled in frustration.

'You know, I once knew a detective, one of the best. He could see things no one else could. He had a younger brother who was knocking off betting shops, left, right and centre. This detective, well, he knew, but he kept it quiet. It was his brother, after all, and family is the strongest bond. Anyway, his brother was eventually arrested after accidentally shooting two people trying to get away, and it soon came out this detective was aware of his crimes all along and didn't say anything. If he had, it would have saved two innocent lives. It cost this detective his job and his life. Lewis, you're a good policeman. You always make the right choice, but if you're covering for her, this isn't going to end well. You need to give her up, for your sake, if not hers.'

Lewis knew Grantham was right. Was he willing to sacrifice his career for this girl? He looked up at the wise old man, closed his eyes and reluctantly nodded.

'You're doing the right thing,' Grantham said, relieved. 'I'll go tell them to bring her in. I suggest you go to the hospital and get your nose checked out. It could be broken.'

Grantham opened the door and stepped out of the room. Lewis waited until he was far enough away and picked up the receiver of a nearby phone. He dialled. He'd given Grantham what he wanted to hear, but there was still time to at least warn Devlin.

#

Devlin rushed around the apartment, pulling clothes from drawers and stuffing them into a duffel bag. She'd already taken care of the videotape, burning the metallic strip in the sink. No one would ever see what she had to do.

She reached under the bed and took out Roxy's metal cigar tin. She flipped open the lid to reveal the large stack of cash springing from it. There was more than enough there to start a new life somewhere else. She stuffed the tin into the duffel bag. As she zipped it up, the phone rang.

She hesitated. She decided it was best not to answer and let it click on to the answering machine. Lewis's voice came through the speaker.

'Devlin, it's Lewis. If you're there, pick up!'

Devlin snatched up the receiver.

'Lewis. I'm here.'

'Devlin, you need to get out of there now. They're coming to arrest you.'

A second after he said that, she could hear the distant sirens getting closer. She peered out the window and saw two squad cars pull up outside.

'Meet me at the drinking fountain in Regent's Park in twenty minutes. Go now,' Lewis said.

Devlin slammed the phone down. She grabbed the duffel bag, slinging it over her shoulder and left the apartment.

When she reached the lobby's front door, police officers appeared on the other side, their silhouettes through the frosted glass, attempting to get inside. She turned, made her way to the other end of a long corridor, and exited via a fire door.

CHAPTER 27

It was a cold night, the frosty air biting at Devlin's skin. She pulled her leather jacket tightly around her as she waited by the drinking fountain hoping Lewis would arrive soon. She heard footsteps behind her and turned, startled, only to relax when she saw Lewis's face.

She dropped the duffel bag on the floor and wrapped her arms around him. A part of her didn't want to let go. It had been so long since she had held someone. She forced herself to release her grip on him. He held out his hand, the charm bracelet in his palm.

'You dropped this,' he said.

She took it with a grateful smile slipping it back over her wrist.

'Thank you. Why are you doing this? I thought you couldn't forgive me for what I'd done.'

'You've suffered enough, and I don't want to be the reason for any more suffering. You remember how I said I once knew someone like you.'

Devlin nodded.

'When she needed me, I wasn't there for her. I failed her. I guess in some ways I'm making amends for that.' Lewis looked at his watch. 'It won't be long before they have police at every airport and train station, so you need to leave now if you want to get away. I'm afraid it's going to have to be a short goodbye.'

'I'll never forget this.'

'I don't think I ever could.'

Devlin gave Lewis one last quick but tight embrace. He threw his arms around her, closing his eyes, trying to savour the moment. He then pushed her away to encourage her to leave.

'There's a taxi waiting at the park entrance, ready to take you where ever you want,' he said. 'Go, before it's too late. I'll try and buy you some more time.'

Devlin smiled as she picked up the duffel bag and slung it back onto her shoulder. She backed away, trying to see as much of Lewis as possible before they were separated forever. Then she turned and walked hastily into the darkness.

#

She stared at the blue and red pencil case in her hands. She was desperate for another fix but knew somewhere Roxy would be disappointed in her. She hadn't been strong enough to resist, and now she was addicted again. Who would help her this time?

She felt claustrophobic in the toilet cubicle, the walls closing in on her like a coffin. The temptation was palpable, and her hands were sweating. She closed her eyes and took a deep breath. She sensed Roxy's presence and a voice inside her head telling her she didn't need help. After all that she had done, she knew she was strong enough. She could survive without it.

She exited the public toilet at the train station, and as she passed by a rubbish bin, she dropped the pencil case inside and didn't look back.

Making her way onto the platform, she wasn't surprised to see two uniformed officers standing guard. She was expecting it. Hopefully, they had yet to be informed of her, and she would slip past unnoticed. After all, what other choice did she have?

She calmly passed by them, and they seemed oblivious to her. She was going to make it. She would be free.

'Excuse me, miss,' she heard one of them say.

She froze. Her heart felt like it was trying to escape her chest. She tried to run, but her muscles had seized. This was the end.

'You dropped your ticket,' he continued.

Devlin turned to see the small stub protruding from his fingers as he extended his hand towards her. Devlin smiled nervously and took the ticket from the officer grinning back.

'Thank you,' she replied.

'Safe journey.'

Devlin quickened her pace down the platform to the waiting train and stepped aboard. She sat down next to a window, the duffel bag perched beside her. The doors closed, and the train began to move. She let out a breath and closed her eyes. She had made it.

It would be a long journey to Brighton, but she had plenty of memories to keep her occupied. Her favourite was of the time she and Roxy sat snuggled on a bench in the park late one evening. They munched on a bag of chips watching the sun go down. Devlin looked up at Roxy and smiled.

'What?' Roxy asked.

'Nothing,' Devlin replied. 'I'm just happy.'

Roxy smiled back, kissing Devlin before snuggling closer together.

Tom Batt is a screenwriter with several film credits to his name. He started writing short stories in 2020 publishing his first collection, *Old Wounds: A Nick Shelby Case*, in 2021 to positive reviews and was followed by a second collection, *MindSpaces* in 2022.

He currently resides in Milton Keynes, UK.

Thank you for taking the time to read this book. I would be grateful if you'd be so kind as to leave a review on Amazon or Goodreads.

Read more stories at
www.toms-tales.com

Follow on social media
Twitter: @picklez4uk
Instagram: @pickles4uk

Printed in Great Britain
by Amazon

25617184R00078